The Return of the Cat

By

Carl S. Kralich

3748 A.D.
The Return of the Cat

By
Carl S. Kralich

©September 2015
TX0008242915

Published by Ruskras Corner
The United States of America

Special Thanks to

The Midnight Chandeliers Critique Group
for support
and the East Texas Writers Guild
for inspiration

3748 A.D. The Return of the Cat - A Karl Sabers Space Knight Adventure
By Carl S. Kralich
ISBN 978-1942542087
First in a series

Character List

On the *Nomad*
Karl Sabers- A student in the colony ship *Nomad*. He is forced out into the universe, little knowing he is destined for greatness.
Denise Sabers- Karl's younger sister. She cannot imagine the fate in store for her after her life is disrupted by space war.
Lightening- A versatile feline, talking is only one of his talents. He does his best to protect his human from harm.
Justin- Son of a grand councilor, he stays beside his companion through thick and thin.
Jacob- Son of a supreme court judge, he is lost when suddenly the world changes around them.
Miss Holo- A holographic teacher program, she is more than just a mundane civil utility.

On the planet Dainare III
Ashley Claymore- An old shopkeeper, he is more invested than anyone realizes.
Isabella- A wolfgirl, she is a faithful slave who never leaves her master.
On the *Crimson Blade*
Surge- A half-alien bounty hunter and commander of the *Crimson Blade*, his eating habits are atrocious, but he has other qualities a girl might like.
Ray- Surge's genius younger stepbrother and the mechanic for the *Crimson Blade*.
B-10- A gynoid navigator, she tries her best among the organics.
Kira- A young Lrakian catgirl who serves onboard the *Crimson Blade*, her happy go lucky nature is countered by her own strength.
Onboard the *Starlight*
Alice- A young Jovian girl who is the engineer onboard the *Starlight*, she wishes for a life away from her home world.
Sophia- An alien slavegirl who is more valuable than her owner knows.

Onboard the *Lady Eris*
Gavorlo Micalo- The captain of The *Lady Eris*, he is a man driven by greed.
Calidi and Ellris- A duo of aliens working with Claymore, with an unknown interest in a mysterious female.
Reginia Craen- A Koal member of the *Lady Eris* crew. Is she good or bad?
Mr. Wilhelm Long- He's 1st mate of the *Lady Eris* & as cold hearted as his captain.
Gavin Hager- A man with a red monocle who acts as *Lady Eris'* mechanic.
Henry Hunter- A former soldier from Io, Jupiter's radio active volcanic moon.
Zrela- An alien member of the *Lady Eris* crew, considered odd among her own kind.
Members of the Syndicate
Baldassara- A high ranking member of the Syndicate.
Nara Crull- Baldassara's right-hand woman.
Thorn- A big cyborg, nothing about him appears good.
In the Neith Federation
Jarl Narkren- Grand Protector of the Neith Federation, he will maintain his government at any cost.
Dergan Fafnir- A Neith agent who is hunting for the threat to his country.
At the High Chapel of Ralethim
Kordova- High theorist of Evlon sect, is he friend or foe?
The Oracle- A self-aware alien artifact with higher ambitions.

Table of Contents

Chapter 1- The Beginning of the End

Have they come to disturb my meal again? the creature wondered as it tried to flex its muscles.

Confined to a cramped cage, it had to be careful not to overturn its precious food. The meager portions were nowhere near enough to satiate the hunger.

Its green eyes with slit-like pupils watched as two humans entered the lab.

Do they not realize the power I possess? Soon my kind will return and all of mankind will serve us once again.

The two humans, each adorned in a white lab coat, turned away from the caged quadropod. It saw its chance.

With its forelimbs, the creature reached through the grill and used its hook-like claws to pull up the latch. It pushed its face against the cage door. The door opened and the orange furred quadropod stepped out.

Ah, freedom.

The old man spun around too late after the cage door opened. "How could you let it escape?!"

"So what." The woman spoke in a relaxed voice. "Specimen-C has been extinct for almost forty years. If someone finds it, they will contact us."

They did not realize that the creature was still in the lab watching them. It waited until their conversation ended.

Another man entered the lab, leaving just enough time for the animal to slip through before the doorway closed. Lurking around a few minutes before it came to an open air vent, which it followed to a mess hall, it pushed the grill up and began the search for food. It started eating food left over from the meal that had ended just a few minutes before. It heard something and got out as quickly as possible.

Walking through the gray hall, it saw two girls talking. The creature ran into a room filled with plastic crates and jumped in one filled with clothes, then fell asleep.

"Where's this going?" one worker asked another, as he shut the lid on the crate without even looking at it.

"The Galaxy Academy," he answered. "Let's get this on the

transport before they dock our pay."

They took the crate and placed it in the cargohold of a shuttle bound to the Galaxy Academy, located within the colony ship, the *Nomad*.

It was the dusk of another century of travel for the *Nomad*, a human generational colony ship. With a population of over 20,000, the forward cylinder was over two miles long and a quarter mile in diameter to accommodate a city built along the inner curve of the rotating chamber, which allowed for artificial gravity.

The *Nomad's* residential section was an almost perfect recreation of Earth's environment with grass and small trees mixed in with the one to six story homes and businesses arranged with the colony.

Between the cylinder and hexagonal hanger section was the Galaxy Academy.

The structure of the Academy consisted of a narrow cylinder with three rings around it. The Galaxy Academy was built to train people from the age of thirteen through nineteen to live and work in space.

The Academy, however, served a darker purpose, preparing the students for a war against the race which had taken Earth from humanity and had forced them into dark space.

While the formerly extinct species from the Station Four cloning lab escaped, the students were returning to the Academy.

"One more year and I graduate." A young man, almost beyond the age of nineteen, spoke to his seventeen-year-old sister.

He was not the kind of person who enjoyed being a student and was happy that his school days would soon be over.

The girl beside him wasn't tall but was very beautiful. She had dark green eyes and long dark brown hair. Despite being siblings, most people did not readily recognize their relation, because his skin was fair whereas hers was almost a light brown.

"Yeah, yeah. You've told me a trillion times already," said the girl, before she put two small black balls in her ears and started listening to music while bobbing her head a bit.

"The shuttle will be leaving artificial gravity," said a voice over the loudspeaker. "Please secure your belongings and prepare for weightlessness."

"I hate this part!" Her muscles tightened.

"Denise, relax," said her brother, with a smile on his face.

6

"Karl, don't talk like that!" she said, before gravity disappeared altogether.

The small black and white shuttle slid along an electromagnetic rail, up from the inner wall of the cylinder towards the axis of the *Nomad*. Once the track leading to the axis ended, the craft used its own power to jump onto the axis rail headed to its destination.

After two hours, the shuttle docked at the Academy and the students exited, dressed in their Academy uniforms.

Most of the girls wore black pants and tank tops underneath an off-the-shoulder shirt with a V-shaped collar. Some of the girls chose to wear miniskirts instead of pants.

The guys were wearing vests over their t-shirts and wore either gray or black pants. The only real variation in the uniform was the color of the shirts.

The boys and girls floated down the broad hallways, all gripping handles meant to pull them along until they reached one of the Academy's rings.

Once they regained their sense of gravity, the two genders went their separate ways. The girls were sent to the gymnasium for their physical examinations, and guys were sent to a marksmanship review.

Karl arrived at the Academy's firing range and found the two students who would become his dorm mates. One of them was a black haired, blue eyed young man and the other was a youth with gray eyes and blonde hair. The dark haired one was John Madison, Karl's closest friend, and gaming partner.

"Hi, John. It's good to see you again." He turned to the other guy. He held out his hand. "Karl Sabers."

"Travis Bowie Crockett." The blonde haired student shook Karl's hand.

You're named after Alamo heroes, Karl thought, having always been a fan of history.

Each student retrieved a pistol consisting partly of a featureless rectangular shaped five-barreled chamber, which housed varying sizes of ammunition. Additionally, an adjustable trigger in the gun's handle activated an ignition circuit which fired the desired round.

As several transparent targets appeared before them, the students raised their weapons and opened fire. Karl shot three holographic humanoids in the head.

They immediately crumbled to pixels.

"So, Travis, what do you like to do?" He placed a block with five holes onto a grip with a trigger. "Are you any good at sword fighting?"

"He's searching for a new sparring partner," stated John. "I'm not very good at it myself."

"Personally, I don't really see why we need combat training," Travis stated. Their targets were altered to resemble the armored alien soldiers who had attacked Earth. "Especially since the forces of the Ruby Eyed Empress have not appeared since our ancestors left Earth."

"Well, it's a tradition." Karl he took aim at the last target, which resembled a red eyed alien with a golden headdress and a black claw in place of her left hand.

The rail car from Station Four departed.

The creature awoke and found itself trapped in a crate. The weightlessness bothered it, but the trip did not last long before the transport arrived at the Academy.

Two men in gray uniforms arrived at the cargohold to collect the shipment.

"What do you want us to do with this?" asked one of the men as he and his coworker picked up the crate.

"Take it to the gym on level ten," the other man answered.

They took the box up the central elevator, then loaded it onto an electric trolley, before guiding it to the gymnasium where the girls were waiting for their gym clothes.

Denise was among the girls waiting. She stood tapping her foot.

Can't they hurry up? I don't want to be stuck here all day.

Not only was she very impatient, she immensely disliked being forced to endure physical examinations right after disembarking from the shuttle.

The two workers unlatched the crate slowly.

"Could you please move faster? We have a gym class to get to," Denise told them, her hands on her hips.

They popped the lid off the crate. Suddenly, a yellow-orange creature jumped out of the crate and took off running before anyone could get a good look at it.

Everyone jumped back. Except Denise.

"That thing was cute!"

"That lizard!" one girl cried.

"It had fur," Denise responded.

"It didn't have fur. It had feathers!" cried another girl.

After gym, Denise sent a message to her brother, which read, "Karl, meet me at lunch. There is something important I have to tell you!"

Three hours later at the mess hall, Karl joined his sister and her two friends, Yuki Amato, and Brittany Bangor. Yuki was an incredibly cute Japanese girl with short black hair, and Brittany was a tall, well-endowed young girl, with long blonde hair.

"What is it?" asked Karl. But Denise didn't have time answer before her friend interrupted.

"Well, I'll tell you," said Brittany with an excited tone of voice. "We saw an orange rat."

"My favorite color," Karl said, sitting back with a smirk on his face. "How big was it?"

"It wasn't a rat. It was a dog!" Yuki responded.

"It wasn't a rat and it wasn't a dog!" Denise said, reentering the conversation. "I don't know what it was. All I know is that it had four legs, a tail, and was as fast as lightning."

"Maybe it was an alien," Karl said as a joke, but nobody laughed. His sister's two friends gave him odd looks. "It was a joke!"

They continued to stare and he felt relieved to leave the girls after being called over by John. His reason for leaving was more embarrassment than a desire to hang out with his friends.

"What a time to be making jokes like that," said Brittany, in an agitated tone.

"What do you mean, time to be making jokes?" Denise asked.

"You haven't heard?" asked Yuki.

"Heard what?" Denise said, crossing her arms.

"About the object coming from the star system ahead of us," said Brittany. "They think it's the real thing."

Denise knew they were referring to the so-called alien spaceship. "What makes them believe it's an actual spacecraft?" Denise asked, as she played with her food.

"Scientists say that the object appears to be metallic," Yuki answered. "And there're rumors that the forces of the Ruby Eyed Empress may be returning."

The girls finished eating and went to their next class.

After class, Karl went down to the museum as he always did. He looked at the old weapons. The M-16 rifle and the 9mm pistol.

Karl had always liked the idea of mechanical guns. He felt they were better than the modern multi-barreled guns, which had all the bullets lined up in each of the different caliber barrels and the gunpowder was ignited through the use of an electrical charge.

Unknown to Karl, the creature from Station Four was watching him.

Karl turned and looked around. He felt as though he was being spied on, but he didn't know by what.

"Is anyone in here?" Karl asked in a loud voice.

"Shh, quiet," a woman's voice said. He turned around and saw the hologram of a woman in glasses. "Do you need something?"

"Yes, is there anyone in here?" Karl asked.

"You are," she answered.

"No, I mean is there anyone besides me?" he asked again.

"I am at your service," she said.

After this, he gave up and left.

He returned to his dorm and saw John and Travis both sitting in their chairs, watching the news.

"Have you heard about the aliens?" John asked.

Karl looked at the video screen.

"What was once one object, is now three!" a news anchor said. "If there were any doubts about this being a real extraterrestrial spacecraft, they are now gone. The question is, have the forces of the Ruby Eyed Empress returned? Now, back to the Takahito scandal."

"All they've talked about is that politician's son." Karl tapped the wall and cut off the news video.

"I was watching that," stated Travis.

"They've been talking about this for three months," Karl said, as he sat down in a chair.

"I'm looking forward to meeting those aliens," John stated.

"Okay, that's nice," Karl said, not taking the alien threat seriously as he pulled out his handheld computer.

"So, what do you guys want to do now?" John asked his two friends.

"I've got a class in the morning," Travis answered, as he got up from his chair. "So, if you don't mind, I'm going to turn in."

"Tomorrow's my day off, so I can sleep late," Karl answered. "How about a duel? I'm a little out of practice."

"I guess," John replied. "Are we going to the Fortress, or are we heading up to the Dome?"

"The Dome," Karl answered. "Unless, you have a problem with it?"

"Nope, let's go," John said.

John and Karl walked into a park complete with trees, grass, and a small pond enclosed within the triangular panels of the gigantic glass dome.

Above them, an image of the Earth shown through the glass as the crowning touch to this arena.

Finally, they reached a wooden bridge built across the fishing pond.

"Same rules as before?" asked Karl, taking a metal rod with a gold disk at its head from his belt.

"On guard!" John said, holding a similar object. A blade of blue light extended from the metal rod in John's hand. John lunged.

Karl touched a small yellow crystal just below the disk, deflecting John's attack with a yellow blade.

Thrusting the golden blade, Karl struck John's chest with the tip of his beam-foil.

The fight lasted a couple of minutes and, for a change, ended in John's victory.

After their battle, the domed garden disappeared leaving John and Karl sitting in their dorm room. Each removed their virtual reality visor.

The next morning Denise went to her history class. She sat down at her desk, which had the equivalent of a laptop computer built right into the top.

A few seconds after all the students took their seats, a female hologram appeared at the front of the room.

The job of education had been passed to computers decades ago after the collapse of the *Nomad's* public education system. The latest form of education was to have humanoid holograms teach the next generation.

"Good morning, Class, I am Hologram 718209. For your convenience, I have been programmed to respond to the name Miss Holo," she stated in a patronizing voice. "Now, can anyone tell me what changes have been made to the Academy?"

Yuki raised her hand. "The Academy's gravity was increased by three percent," she said, as she lowered her hand.

"Well done," Miss Holo replied. "And does anyone understand why?"

Yuki raised her hand, again. "Because the gravity of HD 40307 is believed to be over two and a half times that of Earth," she answered.

"Good and now that we'veeee-eevvvveee-" the hologram continued to hang on the attempted use of a contraction until someone came and shut her off for repairs.

Denise and the other students went out into the hallway and waited for their teacher to be restored to proper working order.

Karl had just returned to his dorm from breakfast and sat down on the bed.

He felt something sharp behind him.

He got up, spun around to see the creature from Station Four asleep on his bed.

He recognized it as an animal he had seen a long time ago in a museum, but he could not remember what it was called.

The creature had long yellow-orange hair all over its body, four legs, a tail, pointy ears, and sharp teeth. It was on its back sleeping with its mouth partly open, its front legs in the air, and its paws bent over its chest.

Karl pulled out his handheld and called his sister.

"Denise," he whispered into his handheld. "I think I found the creature you told me about."

"What is it doing?" she asked.

"He's sleeping," Karl answered.

"How do you know it's a boy?" she asked. "Do you even know

what it is?"

"Yes, but I can't remember what it's called. I'm sending you a picture," he said, as he took the photograph.

Denise's eyes widened. "That's a cat!" she said, in shock as she looked at the image.

"I can't believe I forgot that name," Karl stated. "Oh, and he is definitely a boy."

The cat woke up, jumped off the bed, and began rubbing his scent on Karl.

He looked into the cat's green eyes as he bent down to pet it.

The feline started purring.

"What is that noise?" Denise asked. Karl did not answer. "Karl, are you there?"

"Yes, I'm here," he answered. He scratched the cat's head. "You like that don't you."

"Who are you talking to?" Denise asked.

"Lightening," Karl answered, adding the word under the cat's picture.

"Who's Lightening?" she asked.

"The cat," Karl answered in a cheerful voice. "I thought he should have a name and you said he was fast."

"Lightning doesn't have an *E* in it," she commented.

"Well, it's a name," Karl replied. "It doesn't have to be spelled the same."

"They've got my history teacher back online, so I'll have to go," she said.

"Don't tell anyone about Lightening," Karl said, in a concerned voice.

"Of course. I won't tell anyone. Talk to you later, bye," Denise said, as she shut off her handheld and went back to class.

She and the other students sat down, and the teacher reappeared.

"Good morning, Class. I am Hologram 718209. For your convenience I have been programmed to respond to the name Miss Holo," she stated again.

Most of the students were upset that they were going to repeat the same lesson.

"Now, can anyone tell me what changes have been made to the Academy?"

"A 0.3 increase in gravity." Yuki answered without having her hand raised as she did the first time.

"Raise your hand next time," said the Hologram. "And does anyone understand why?" She looked around the room. "Anyone?"

Yuki raised her hand, this time. "Because HD 40307 is a heavy world," she answered. "Following the Koal invasion of Earth, the surviving orbital colonies were configured into generation."

There was a loud buzz heard in the room. The hologram disappeared and the students ran out of the classroom, after downloading the notes to their handhelds.

Denise and Yuki started walking together back to their dorm. Then Denise got a message on her handheld from Karl.

"Denise, I need you to come meet me at my dorm. I will let you in so you can meet Lightening."

"I better not get busted for this," Denise muttered.

"Who's Lightening?" Yuki asked, after she read the message over Denise's shoulder.

"You'll see when we get to my brother's dorm," she told her.

"You know that girls aren't allowed in the boys' dorms!" Yuki reminded her.

"Oh, just come on!" Denise said, as she dragged Yuki off to her brother's dorm.

Karl was resting on a couch in the sitting area of his dorm. Lightening padded into the room and jumped onto the sofa.

The cat then walked onto Karl's chest.

"So, you wanted to come visit me. You're such a sweet cat," he said, as Lightening began to nuzzle him.

Then there was a buzz at the door. "Denise, is that you?"

He scratched Lightening's ears.

"Yeah, the goose is at the door," said Denise. Their father often called her 'Goose' when they were kids.

Lightening's ears perked up. It almost looked like he was smiling.

"Come in!" Lightening said, assuming that food was on the way.

"Um, Karl, who is that?" Denise asked. The voice she heard was not her brother's normal tone.

Can't tell her the cat just spoke, she's going to think I'm crazy, Karl thought to himself. "Uh, that was me!" he lied. "Come in."

The door slid open and he was surprised to see Yuki there as well.

Lightening gave them an angry glare. *I've been cheated out of a goose.*

"That's a cat!" Yuki said in shock.

"Is that cat glaring at us?" Denise asked. Lightening started to swing his tail back and forth.

Karl looked at him. "I think he is. Doesn't he look so cute?" Karl answered. His sister glared at him a bit.

"This is amazing! Where did you get him?" Yuki asked.

"He was the creature that was in our gym clothes," Denise told her.

"He's the one who found me," Karl answered.

"We got to tell somebody about this!" Yuki said, staring intently at the cat.

"NO!" the Sabers siblings said together.

"Not no, but hel- Ow!" Karl yelled as Denise slapped him on the arm. "Why did you do that?!"

"No cussing! You know I don't like it!" she reminded him.

"All right, all right!" he said, rubbing his arm, which turned red.

"I think we should tell Commander Kouldntnam about the cat," Yuki told them.

"His name is Lightening," Karl informed her. "You know what they might do to him if anyone finds out?"

"Well, they would probably find a way to make more cats like him," she answered.

"Probably by dissecting him," Karl stated. Lightening started swinging his tail even faster. "He looks upset."

"What makes you think he's upset?" Denise asked.

"He just has that look on his face," answered Karl. Lightening did have a perturbed expression.

"Well, you don't plan on keeping him here?" Yuki asked.

"Yes," he answered, as he scratched the cat's head. "That's what I'm planning."

"How are you going to take care of him?" Yuki asked.

"I'm going to feed him, brush him, and clean up after him," Karl answered. "Denise had a dog when we were kids. I read cats were much easier to take care of."

"I miss Pepper," Denise said, being reminded of her dog who had

15

died a few years back.

"By the way, have you heard anything about the alien ship?" Karl asked, trying to distract Yuki from the idea of telling somebody about Lightening.

"Yes, I have. It's speeding up," she answered. "It's moving twice as fast as it was earlier."

"So, do you think these are good aliens or bad aliens?" he asked.

"I've got no idea, but I have an awfully bad feeling about this," answered Denise, just before her handheld started playing music. She picked it up and Brittany's face appeared. "I have to take this." Denise left the room.

"Well, they have a ship that was able to reach us out here in deep space," stated Yuki. "So, scientists believe they've probably moved beyond things like war and violence."

"Somehow I doubt that. They could be coming to invade," Karl said. He picked up Lightening and held him in his arms like a baby.

Lightening put his paws on Karl's chest. "Now, let's get back to the important subject."

Gripping Karl's vest with his paw, the cat extended himself towards the human's face, looking him in the eye. "I'm hungry."

"Karl, this isn't the time to be thinking about food," Denise said as she walked back in. "And please stop changing your voice, and how come you're able to do that now? You've never done that before in our whole lives."

"All right, none of us is to say anything to anyone about the cat," Karl said.

He pulled the cat off of him.

Karl was now covered in cat hair.

"Can we tell Brittany?" Denise asked.

"No," he answered.

"Why not?" Yuki asked.

"Because I don't want anyone else knowing about him yet," he answered.

Yuki looked at her handheld. "It's almost time for math class."

"No, I don't want to go!" Denise yelled.

"You have to go, don't you want a B?" Yuki asked.

"Fine. Bye, Karl," Denise said. She and Yuki walked out the door.

"Sayonara," Yuki said, bowing to him.

"Bye," he said as he waved his hand. The door shut and Karl turned to the cat. "Do you understand me?"

"Yes. What's for lunch?" Lightening asked.

"I thought animals couldn't talk," he said.

"You who are ignorant of the whole universe, are questioning the talking cat," Lightening said, as he scratched his ear with his back paw. "And I still haven't been fed yet."

"What do cats eat, anyway?" Karl asked. "We have some carrots and celery, and there might be some leftover egg rolls."

"I'm a carnivore," Lightening stated. "I eat mice, birds, and fish. Preferably stuff that still has a lot of liquid to it."

Karl went to the dorm fridge to fetch the cat a can of tuna, and Lightening inhaled it.

"It's a lot better than the food those other men were giving me."

Lightening licked his paws.

"What other men?" Karl asked.

"Those men definitely did not like cats," Lightening said, as he rubbed his scent on Karl, "because they never once petted me."

"What did the men look like?" Karl asked, as he lifted Lightening up in his arms.

"They were ordinary looking humans that wore white coats. One of them might have been a female," Lightening answered.

"Now it makes sense. Station Four has been cloning extinct animals for a long time," Karl said. He scratched Lightening's ear. "It's about time they brought back something useful."

"I agree. I'm hungry."

"I already fed you."

"No you didn't," Lightening said, as he jumped out of Karl's arms.

"Fine, I was planning on having lunch anyway," he said, as they went towards the refrigerator.

"I still can't believe you want to keep that thing," John said, glancing over at Karl, who was sitting on the couch with Lightening.

"But he's so sweet," Karl replied, while scratching the cat's right ear.

Karl was not able to keep Lightening a secret from John and Travis for very long, but he would be able to keep both of them quiet about the cat.

"What do you do when the cat needs to go to the bathroom?" John asked.

"You know, that stuff they use to line children's playgrounds," Karl answered. "That used to be something called cat litter."

"How do you know all this?" asked Travis

"I had to write a paper on it," Karl answered.

"It's your fault for taking all those extra history classes," John commented.

"Speaking of the cat," said Travis, pulling out his handheld. "You know what time it is?"

Karl reluctantly pulled out his handheld and transferred fifty credits into each of his friends' student bank accounts. "Now your lips are sealed about him, right?"

"Of course," Travis answered.

"Now I can get that new game," John commented.

You better be worth this, Karl thought, looking down at the cat.

Lightening began purring on Karl's lap.

The alien ships had grown even closer to the *Nomad*, and the Grand Council had come together to discuss the situation with the aliens. Their hope was to establish contact with the visitors. However, their history with the aliens had not been a pleasant one.

All students were put on alert and ordered to take another firearm training class prior to the aliens' arrival.

Also, the upcoming Halloween party at the Galaxy Academy had been changed to a military theme. Each of the students was expected to be armed in the event of war.

"So, Karl, who are you planning to take to the ball," asked Travis, as several transparent targets appeared before him. He shot three shadowy humanoids in the head. They immediately crumbled to pixels.

"Well, I'm not going with anyone," he answered, placing a chamber block onto a grip with the trigger. "I do plan on meeting up with Yuki and spending most of my time with her."

"You're lucky to have a girlfriend," John stated. "And she's as much of a nerd as you and I are."

"Well, there's always Denise, she's into most of the same things." Karl took aim at the transparent figures.

"She doesn't really like video games. Besides I can't make heads or tails of that anime stuff."

"Well. I can't help, then," Karl said. "If you need something to talk to Denise about, Travis can download the Bleak mangas to your handheld."

"Why don't you get Travis to date her?" John asked, with a bit of a depressed look on his face.

"By the way," said Travis, trying to change the subject. "Karl, didn't you get a new pistol?"

"Yes, I did." Karl walked over to his bag and pulled out a .45 caliber automatic pistol.

"Where'd you get that antique?" asked John.

"My father sent it to me," Karl answered. "He thought-"

"Attention, all students, please retire for the night," said a voice over the intercom. "Due to the current situation regarding the unidentified object, students will not be permitted to leave their dorms after 2100 hours, and power shall be cut off at 2200 hours."

"Lovely," Karl said, under his breath. "Guess that puts an end to our late night gaming."

Meanwhile, in a room occupied by Denise and her dorm mates...

"So, Yuki. What are you planning to go to the party as?" Denise asked while relaxing on her bed.

"Well, the rules say that we have to dress up as something from our native culture." She finished buttoning her pajama top. "So, I was thinking of dressing as a female samurai."

Denise sighed and sat up. "You Japanese are lucky that you have cool things in your culture," said Denise, in a disappointed voice. "There is nothing cool for girls to dress up as in my culture."

"Well, dress as a guy," Yuki suggested. "You could always dress as a soldier, a pirate, a cow-"

Denise suddenly looked furious.

"Yuki!" she said gritting her teeth. "Do you remember how I feel about WESTERN THINGS?!" She grabbed her pillow and hurled it at Yuki, knocking her to the side.

The bathroom door slid open and Brittany walked into the room wearing nothing but a towel.

"What's going on out here?" she asked, having heard Denise's scream.

"We were just discussing our costumes for the party," Yuki said, as she got off the floor. "Denise got a little carried away."

"And just what do you mean by that?" yelled Denise.

"Attention all students, please retire for the night," said a voice over the intercom. "Due to the current situation regarding the unidentified object, students will not be permitted to leave their dorms after 2100 hours, and power shall be cut off at 2200 hours."

"Great, that's just what we need," stated Denise.

October 31st finally arrived and everyone was getting ready for the party.

Karl dressed up as a gangster from the 1920s. John dressed as an American soldier from World War I. Travis was dressed in his usual clothes with coonskin hat, a saber, and a bowie knife.

Denise was dressed as a pirate. Brittany was dressed as an Amazon with a short sword that had an inward curved cutting edge. Yuki chose to wear a long white dress with poufy sleeves that had bow decor and a choker collar. Her black hair was covered by a thin veil and in her right hand was a dagger.

"Where did you find that?" asked Brittany, looking at the pearls lining the dress.

"Oh, I saw it on the cover of an old book Karl gave me and had it made," Yuki answered. "It was called *Murder as the Organist Plays* published in 2015, almost two thousand years ago."

"What's an organist?" asked the blonde.

"I don't know," Yuki replied. "I'll have to ask Karl again. He loves all that ancient historical stuff."

The anomaly that stood out like a sore thumb among all the

costumes was the same generic looking pistol that resembled a brick with a handle.

Karl walked into the large area decorated with items from different cultures.

He saw Denise and Yuki standing next to a blonde woman who was tall. She was dressed in the plain gray uniform of a United Earth Forces soldier from before the invasion of Earth.

"Good for nothing child," said the woman.

"What did you just call me?!" said Denise, turning to the woman.

"Little brat, you have no idea what culture is," she stated.

Denise would have loved to have taken out her gun and shot her, but killing her would not solve the problem.

Many of the people on board the *Nomad* were just like that woman, devoted to the idea that their people and culture were more important than the individual.

"I prefer it when people do not insult my sister," Karl said to the woman, with his arms crossed.

"Figures that you would dress as a criminal as well," said the woman, with her arms crossed and her eyes closed. After not hearing a reply, she opened her eyes and saw that Karl was dragging Denise and Yuki away from her.

She believed that they left out of weakness, but Karl left because the conversation was annoying. So, he decided to save his sister and Yuki from wasting time fighting with that woman.

"So, how is Lightening doing?" Yuki asked. Karl stood there and looked off to the side. "Did something bad happen to him?"

"No. He's all right," Karl answered. "But I'm going broke just trying to feed him."

Karl and Yuki walked over to the food table and saw Lightening standing on the table devouring a bowl of tuna salad.

Karl grabbed the cat and picked him up.

However, Lightening had hooked his claws into the white tablecloth and all the objects on the table were dragged with the cat.

Lightening then flipped around in Karl's hands and sank his claws into Karl's right shoulder.

"What's Lightening doing here?" asked Yuki.

"Isn't it obvious," Lightening stated, as he began nuzzling Karl's neck. "I snuck out."

Yuki did not hear Lightening's statement.

She and most of the other girls had crowded around the doors as Justin Nemic, dressed as a Scandinavian prince, and Jacob Conweell, dressed as a politician from the colonial era, entered the room.

Justin Nemic was a blonde haired, blue eyed son of Chase Nemic, the European Grand Councilor. Jacob Conweell was the dark haired son of Madam Supreme Court Judge, Carson Conweell. As the children of politicians, they were part of the idolized group that existed on board the *Nomad*.

Yuki totally abandoned Karl.

"That's not fair, Yuki's my girl," Karl stated.

"She prefers them to you?" Lightening sniffed the air.

"They're politician's sons."

"So, become one of those so she will like you."

"I would be a good politician but a person practically has to be born into politics to be a politician."

"If you're that worried about it. Fight. Show them who's boss." Lightening licked Karl's neck,

"I can't do that," Karl replied. "Most girls don't approve of violence."

"Strange, all the females I've known in my past lives were pretty violent," said the cat, before he bit Karl on the side of his neck.

"Ow, Lightening," Karl said, as he continued to pet the cat. "What do you mean past lives?"

"People on this ship sure are stupid," Lightening stated. "Cats have nine lives, haven't you ever heard of the cat food brand?"

"And what happens after your ninth life?" Karl asked.

"We lie down with lambs," he answered.

"Karl!" said a voice from behind him. He turned to see his sister standing there with a perturbed expression on her face. "Why you did bring Lightening here?"

"Here," Karl said, pulling the cat off of him and holding Lightening in front of Denise. "Ask him."

"Well, Lightening, how did you get here?" she asked in a sarcastic tone.

"Meow," was his answer.

Karl turned Lightening around and looked him straight in the eye. "Why must you always cause me trouble?"

Lightening started purring like an engine.

"I love you, too." Karl brought Lightening to his shoulder and hugged him.

"Looks like my brother has found true love," Denise said, as she left the man-cat soap opera.

She now had to figure out what she was going to do. *Brittany and Yuki are panting over those two idiots*. She glanced over at the stage, where they were preparing to broadcast the meeting between the aliens and the world leaders.

A loud growl suddenly went through the ears of everyone in the room.

Denise turned to see Justin restraining her brother and Jacob trying to get Lightening off his face. He pulled Lightening off and threw him at the wall.

The cat hit the wall feet first, then jumped on the floor and ran into the crowd. Karl's hands were bound and he was dragged away by two security guards.

After everyone had calmed down and the party resumed. Yuki and Brittany sat down with Denise in the hope of making her feel a little better.

"Karl didn't do anything," Denise said, gritting her teeth. "Those sons of-"

"Denise, I feel the same way," Yuki interrupted. "But there's nothing we can do about it now. We're just going to have to wait and see what happens."

An image of the giant black alien ship appeared on the wall behind the stage. The port and starboard were part of a large V-shaped wing attached to the stern. Within the V-shaped wing was a long cylinder with two horn-like objects running all the way to the diamond shaped bow.

The large ship was escorted by two long black triangular ships with yellow stripes running along the edge of the vessels. On the stern of the escort ships were short backward swept wings with long rods attached to them.

Karl sat across a large desk from Commander Kouldntnam, who was an obese man with a grim expression on his face.

"So, Mr. Sabers," he said, with a disappointed tone in his voice.

"How long have you been in possession of that animal?"

Karl didn't really know what to say about the situation and remained silent.

"You understand that stealing a research animal is a felony with a twenty-year sentence."

"I didn't steal him," he stated.

"The fact that the subject was in your possession is enough to convict you," said Kouldntnam. "However, due to it being the eve of contact and this being your first offense, we can afford to overlook this." He looked Karl straight in the eye. "If you are willing to help us find this creature-"

"What will happen if you find him?" asked Karl, worrying about what might happen if Lightening was taken back to the lab.

"The cat will be handed back to its creators for further research."

"I won't be going back," said a voice, which Karl instantly recognized as Lightening.

"What was that?" asked Kouldntnam.

Lightening jumped on Kouldntnam's desk.

Kouldntnam jumped back in shock. "What is this?!"

Karl stood up and looked at the cat. "This is Lightening," he stated as Lightening wiped his face with his paw.

"I do not like the way you have been treating my person," said the cat. He licked his hind leg. "You can treat another cat's property any way you like, but he is mine."

Before Karl could react there was a loud noise.

The larger spaceship docked with the *Nomad* and the alien occupants were met by a squad of *Nomad's* soldiers dressed in gray and black uniforms.

The Koal appeared as humanoids encased in black armor with jet black coats worn over the armor, looking like something out of a history lesson. Their helmets were somewhat of a diamond shape with the edges rounded off. A single spike rose from the top of their helmets. The only color came from the triangular gold buckles on their coats and the red slot in their helmets, which appeared to cover their alien eyes.

As the soldiers approached the Koal, armed with their rectangular shaped rifles, one of the Koal removed a small round object from his coat.

A strange pulse emitted from the spherical object, and the alien warriors pulled out black curved pistols.

The humans attempted to open fire, but no shots came out as the soldiers frantically squeezed the triggers of their disabled weapons. The ignition circuits were completely fried.

Before they could consider retreat, the *Nomad's* forces were gunned down by bolts of yellow light.

In a matter of minutes, the Koal swept through the Galaxy Academy, which now became the primary target of their invasion. Three Koal entered the room where the students were holding their party.

Each of the aliens carried a crystal weapon which was the size of a pistol, with a red handgrip. The black armored invaders opened fire on the students, who dropped to the floor unconscious after being stunned by blue pulses of energy.

Denise hurled her now useless firearm at one of the Koal. While he was distracted, she ran at him and grabbed one of the curved blaster pistols from under his now open coat. She fired a gold shot at him, but his black armor absorbed the blast. She squeezed the trigger several more times, but nothing came out.

The armored Koal grabbed her by the neck and lifted her into the air, then choked her until she passed out.

Alarms rang out as the invaders overran the Academy, stunning the people and dragging them back to the alien ship.

After incapacitating most of the students at the party, one of the invaders made his way through the hallway to Kouldntnam's office. He lunged into the room and found Karl, Lightening, and Kouldntnam.

A purple flash came from a black sphere in the Koal's left hand as Kouldntnam drew his multi-barrel pistol and aimed it at the alien.

The Koal shot Kouldntnam, then discarded the gun.

Karl reached into his jacket and drew the .45 pistol and fired three times at the stranger. A cold mist emerged from the cracked armor, as the alien dropped to the ground dead.

Karl walked over to the dead Koal on the floor and removed the coat and weapons from his fallen enemy.

Chapter 3- Retaliation

As the two smaller Koal ships fired upon the *Nomad's* residential section, a large object rose from the stern of the generation ship. The human battleship resembled a rocket with a large ring section at her stern and was over 1.5 kilometers in length matching the wingspan of the alien mothership. Eight missiles launched from the deck of the battleship. The foreign ships fired several plasma blasts at the warhead like firing a shotgun at a volley of arrows.

One missile detonated prematurely upon contact with the plasma and vaporized four others. The alien battleships were bathed in a single white flash.

Whatever sense of relief the battleship crew had vanished when the two ships emerged from the explosion intact.

The bow of the human battleship split open revealing the tip of a rail gun. The weapon fired and a trail of blue flames followed the projectile, striking the starboard side of one of the smaller alien ships, tearing the vessel apart. The second alien battleship continued firing upon the Terran ship.

Denise awoke to find herself in a cell with thirteen other girls including her friends, Yuki, and Brittney.

"Are you okay?" Yuki asked, with a worried tone in her voice. "Are you still in pain?"

"Yes," she answered as she rubbed her bruised neck. "Some alien was trying to strangle me." She got up and looked around. The walls of the cell appeared to be constructed of bronze and the entrance to the cell was covered by a thick sheet of glass. Some of her cellmates were crying, others sitting quietly staring straight ahead, their eyes dull and listless. A few tried to comfort each other in small groups.

Will we live or die? Denise wondered to herself. *Has everyone been captured? Dear Father, please help us.*

Everyone in the cell was filled with despair.

Would they become slaves?

Test subjects?

Or something worse?

"What happened since I got knocked out? Any news about my brother and the others?"

"I don't know," answered Yuki. "They took us aboard their ship. We've been separated since the invasion."

Three Koal proceeded down the corridor towards the cell, each dragging an unconscious girl behind them.

They tossed the girls in the cell and walked off.

"They got most of us at the party," Brittany stated, "but they seem to bring more here as they find them."

Denise then continued on praying in silence.

As the aliens continued to collect any humans they came across, Karl and Lightening took off running as another Koal followed them. They ran down the hall and hopped on a trolley and rode it to the museum section of the Academy.

It did not take long for the Koal to catch up with the teenager and the cat.

The Koal drew his blaster pistol and fired it at Karl.

However, the black coat that he was now wearing absorbed the blast.

Karl returned fire.

The shot went through the armor of the Koal, killing him.

Karl was relieved that he made it out of his first run-in with two alien enemies.

Karl opened fire at the glass window covering a display of twentieth-century firearms. He grabbed two extra magazines from the exhibit, stuffed them in his pocket, then grabbed an AK-47.

As he loaded his new weapon, he noticed two figures out of the corner of his eye.

Fortunately before he had a chance to open fire, he realized they were students just like himself. However to his disappointment, it turned out to be Justin and Jacob, two of the last people he would have wanted to have at his side.

"You there!" Karl cried out. There were no other options. He would need their help to fight the Koal.

"Sabers, what are you doing?" Jacob asked, looking at Karl like a madman. "Our weapons won't work on the aliens."

"Anything without a battery will work," answered Karl, as he cocked his rifle. "The antiques seem to work fine, and their coats will protect us from their own weapons. Grab as many weapons as you can carry and when you kill a Koal, take its jacket."

Jacob stripped the black coat from the alien's body just as Karl had done, and he and Justin took rifles for themselves.

Between the three of them, they had six rifles, four shotguns, three submachine guns, and at least a dozen pistols of different calibers.

Karl considered grabbing a Civil War era cannon and a World War II Japanese katana but determined that these weapons were far too impractical to take with them.

The three students made their way back to Kouldntnam's office in hopes of accessing the Academy's camera systems. Jacob occupied the dead commander's chair and attempted to access the computer systems.

"Fingerprint identification required," flashed on the screen.

Karl and Justin immediately grabbed the corpse of the computer's previous owner and pressed his dead thumb against a panel on the side of the keyboard. And to their surprise, they discovered not only was the invasion force limited almost entirely to the Academy, but the aliens were actually outnumbered five to one in favor of students.

"Why would an invasion force be so outnumbered?" Justin asked, looking at Jacob.

"Because bad guys are stupid," Lightening answered, rubbing himself against Karl's leg.

"They must be entirely relying on the idea that all weapons need a power source," Karl concluded.

This meant that their small resistance might not be just a final stand, but they might actually succeed in holding back or even have a chance of driving out the alien forces.

Watching the Academy security camera, the trio noticed several dozen students moving along in one of the hallways nearby. Escorting the students were two Koal warriors. Seeing this as an excellent opportunity to increase their numbers, the three of them went to liberate their comrades.

Karl switched his rifle to semiautomatic. As the first enemy came within range, he fired a single shot.

Cold mist rose from the cracked helmet of the dead alien. Seeing his comrade fall, the other alien raised his weapon but was gunned down before he had a chance to fire.

"Karl!" exclaimed a voice from the crowd. Karl turned to see his friend, John. "You escaped? What's going on?"

"You've just been drafted," Karl answered, handing his friend a rifle. "We're taking back the Academy."

"My fellow humans." Justin addressed the group as weapons were distributed to the students. "We now face the very same enemies who stole the Earth from our ancestors, and now seek to take the only home we've ever known. If mankind is to survive, we must drive the alien scourge from…"

"Is he just going to stand there and give a speech in the middle of an alien invasion?" Lightening asked, jumping on Karl's shoulders. "Hot air must run in the family."

"I think so," Karl said, agreeing with the cat.

The weapons were divided among the students, and those who were unarmed were sent to the museum section with Jacob to retrieve more weapons.

The original group, including Karl, John, and Justin, continued making their way through the halls of the Academy.

This is what they had been training for.

The day when the Koal would return and they would be forced to defend their home from the race that stole Earth from their ancestors.

As the students walked by the blasted open door of a classroom, a familiar light appeared at the front of the room.

"Good morning Class, I am Hologram 718209 for your convenience I have been programmed to respond-" Miss Holo paused. "What has happened to the classroom?"

Great, it's just the teacher program, Karl thought, about to turn away from the classroom.

"What good is the teacher going do?" asked John. "We're under attack."

"My base program was initially engineered as a tactical AI," the holographic teacher commented. "My storage requirement is only one petabyte."

"I guess we might be able to use her," Justin stated pulling out his handheld. "I should have enough space on here."

"All right, go ahead," Karl said.

"So he is going to be keeping a woman inside of his pocket," Lightening stated. "I'm sure there's nothing strange about that."

29

Chapter 4- Captured

A different group of students proceeded towards the alien vessel, opening fire at every alien they saw.

"What's going on?" Emerging from a storage closet, Travis shouted over gun bursts.

"Join us! It's war!" Jacob answered. "The war our forefathers fled from has finally come. We're fighting back."

Travis abandoned his cramped hiding place with enthusiasm.

As before, the liberated students looted the jackets of the Koal and weapons were passed to the new recruits.

Under Jacob's command, the students charged into the boarding tube of the alien vessel.

As they entered into a black corridor lined with dim blue triangular fixtures, a small force of aliens was mowed down as they attempted to intercept the students.

Without warning, a series of doors slammed down from the ceiling and trapped the humans.

The air became thin in the section where they were trapped.

"Approximately two dozen students under Jacob Conweell have been captured," said Miss Holo.

"What?!" Karl questioned, looking at Justin's handheld. "What happened?"

"Sabers, how could you let this happen?!" Justin complained.

"Sure, blame the guy who rescued you," Lightening commented, wiping his face with his paw.

"Look," Karl said, staring Justin directly in the eye. "We just need another strategy. So far they're only trying to capture, not kill us."

"We need a new strategy," said John.

"That's what the hologram's for," said the cat.

"Any ideas?" asked Karl.

"Calculating," Miss Holo replied. "I might be able to overtake their systems if I could make direct contact with the mothership's servers."

"How do we do that?" asked Justin.

"One of you would have to get me close enough to upload myself," she answered. "The mothership has to be dealt with.

Otherwise, it's possible they may target the residential section of the *Nomad*."

Unexpectedly, a floating black sphere drifted into the room.

The students turned their weapons on the alien device and began firing.

The bullets curved around the object as the sphere split open, revealing a blue gem which immediately emitted a blue flash.

Karl and the other humans collapsed on the ground, unconscious.

Only a few moments later they were dragged off by the Koal to their ship.

With the two smaller alien vessels destroyed and the students subdued, the Koal mothership detached itself from the *Nomad* before the human warship could fire its railgun.

The starless pocket of space appeared before the spaceship and the vessel launched itself into the void.

Chapter 5- Alone in Space

In all, 549 humans had been taken by the Koal after the attack on the Galaxy Academy.

The ventilation shaft leading to the bridge popped open and a small yellow-orange tabby with a wrist watch in his mouth dropped down from the ceiling.

Lightening made his way undetected by the armored aliens. The cat jumped onto a panel with color coded crystals. Then Lightening dropped the watch onto the control panel.

"First touch the amber crystal," said the voice of Miss Holo coming from the watch in a pitch that could not be detected by the aliens. "Now press the blue one, followed by the turquoise, that should trigger the self destruct."

Lightening jumped down underneath the control panel and began licking his paws.

Alarm lights and sirens, too high pitched for Terran ears, sounded throughout the ship. The armored aliens began to panic and rushed to their escape pods or small attack craft, leaving their prisoners behind.

Karl awoke to find himself on the bronze floor of a cell. He lifted himself up on one elbow.

However, being too dazed to worry about anything, he slid down and went back to sleep.

"We lost to those monsters," said an unpleasantly familiar voice. Karl awoke and turned his head to see Justin standing there among the students seated on the floor. "They took Earth without a fight and now they are taking us to some dark corner of the universe."

Several of his fellow male students were in the room. He looked around but didn't see Travis or John.

Did they manage to escape somehow?

From what Karl could tell, most of the men with him in the cell kept their heads down, giving impressions they were feeling sorry for themselves.

At that point, Karl remembered everything that had happened. There was almost no chance of him ever seeing his family again. As far as people on the *Nomad* were concerned, he might as well be dead. He realized that the *Nomad* could've easily been destroyed by the alien ship.

Is there really any point to- his nihilistic thought was quickly interrupted by the sound of stampeding armored figures passing beside his cell.

"What happened?" Karl asked aloud, as the male students jumped up dumbfounded.

Their guards just vanished without warning as strange lights flashed on and off throughout the ship.

After what seemed like an eternity, the glass door covering their cell slid open and some of the students stepped out into the hallway of the vessel.

The crowd erupted into pandemonium as many immediately began seeking their close friends and loved ones while others, panicking, disappeared into the seemingly endless dark corridors of the ship.

"Karl!" said a familiar voice.

Karl turned to see his sister still dressed in her pirate costume rush towards him through the crowd. "Denise, you're all right!"

"Attention, all students," said a voice coming over the intercom. "This is Miss Holo, otherwise known as Hologram 718209. At this time, the situation is under control and would Karl Sabers, Jacob Conweell, and Justin Nemic, please report to the bridge immediately."

When they arrived, they found a group of three humans who were not students of the Academy but were part of the *Nomad's Council.* The first was an old Asian woman and beside her were two white men.

"Congratulations," said one of the men. "You three have accomplished your duty. At this moment, you are considered-"

"I called them here," Miss Holo's voice interrupted from the alien control panel. "They were the ones who-"

"Protocol 59," said the other male councilor. "Disable AI personality and engage emergency tactical role."

"Affirmative," Miss Holo's now monotone voice replied. "Martial law will commence, and genetic compatibility subroutines will be completed in 0500 hours."

"What did you do to her?!" Justin asked. The others stood there in a state of shock.

"Why'd you do that?!" Karl demanded.

"This is what she was created for originally," said the female councilor. "In a matter of hours the AI will have complete control over this vessel. As such, this vessel will become the ark that will take us to a new world."

"Shouldn't we try to get back the *Nomad*?" Karl asked, hoping there was still a chance those aboard *Nomad* might have survived.

"Conweell, Nemic," said one male councilor. "I trust that we can depend on you to ensure the survival of humanity and that you would not do anything to jeopardize the continuation of our species."

Justin and Jacob saluted the man.

"Good, you two may leave now."

As Justin and Jacob turned to leave, the three councilors directed their attention towards Karl Sabers.

"The *Nomad* is on a one way course towards HD 40307, which may already be occupied by the forces of the Ruby Eyed Empress," one of the councilors answered. "Even if the *Nomad* were allowed to continue and able to establish a colony it would still be centuries before that ship arrives."

"But-" Karl attempted to interject, feeling it more practical to integrate the alien technology with their own.

"The chances of humanity's survival are greater if we can establish our own colony," the other male councilor interrupted.

"Does this student have any family onboard?"

"Only known sibling, Denise Sabers," Miss Holo replied.

"If you intend on your sister and yourself surviving," the councilor continued, "you will follow our directive, and look only to a new world built for our future."

Karl was about to say something else when he saw the light reflect off the green eyes of a small creature lurking in a corner.

Is there nothing else I can do? Karl thought to himself, now coming to the realization that his life was now in the hands of those standing before him.

He reluctantly saluted to the three councilors before turning to leave.

Several hours later the students were instructed to meet in the main cargohold of the ship.

Lightening followed them as they headed down the narrow black corridors lined with dim blue triangular light fixtures that lit the way.

The two male students entered the large auditorium, where they were joined by a great multitude of their peers.

Most of the students were still dressed in their costumes.

Standing before them upon a temporary stage constructed from alien crates were the three remaining members of *Nomad*'s Grand Council.

Councilor Johnson stepped up to the makeshift podium.

"My fellow humans," he addressed the crowd. "This is a tragic time for all of us. We have all lost that which was most important to us, whether it be our community, our friends, our comrades, our families, or our homes. It may be likely that we are the only humans left in the universe. As such it is our duty to preserve both our species and the many cultures that come from the world we lost. Therefore, it has been determined by the Grand Council, that we shall use this ship to continue our mission to seek out a new home, where we can begin again."

He stepped down and allowed the female councilor, Ashya Sanders, to take the stand.

"To manage our scarce resources," she began. "We shall divide the population into groups of six. These groups will be given an area of the ship and some rations will be supplied to each group."

So with those words, most of the population was divided into groups of six with an even number of male and female counterparts, who were matched for genetic compatibility.

The group containing Karl, Justin, and Jacob had three tall blonde haired, well-endowed girls as members, Brittany Bangor, Lily Doyle, and Eva White, together they constituted the group labeled 58-A.

Chapter 6- The Missing Girl

Over the next several weeks, life went relatively smoothly for 58-A and the other 91 groups onboard the ship.

Each group took turns learning how to operate the ship. And the food stolen from the Academy by the aliens was holding up fairly well.

The only problems that occurred with group 58-A over that several weeks involved Karl Sabers.

Unlike most of the other students, he still wore the black coat of the Koal over his uniform, which often angered his peers.

He did not express any interest in seeking friendships with anyone.

Since the attack on the *Nomad*, he seemed to spend most of his time with Lightening.

A cat.

Karl even shared his food with the cat, which resulted in his semi-chubby appearance fading into that of a thin dark figure.

"Karl!" said the angry voice of Denise.

Karl huddled in the corner of the large room that had been assigned to his group.

"Get out of the emo-corner or I'm going to have to beat you out of it!"

Karl did not reply.

"Stop sulking." She grabbed the collar of her brother's shirt. "You can't just give up now! The Lord delivered us from the Koal-"

Lily ran over to the siblings and slapped Denise on the cheek before the latter could finish her statement.

"How can you believe in Someone who could allow our world to fall?!"

However, one of the things Denise had never quite gotten down was the part about "turning the other cheek".

Denise raised her hand and slapped Lily three times as severely as she had been struck.

"I'm only stating the truth," said Denise. "If anything, you should be thanking God that you're still alive."

The fact that Denise's faith had not been lost with the *Nomad* created a barrier of hostility between her and the other students, even to the point that her closest friends were starting to avoid her.

This included Brittany, who had been one of Denise's best friends and roommates for the last few years.

Denise started backing away, then turned to look at her brother. "Don't forget that I'm here for you, Karl."

She left her brother alone.

He had never said a word to her.

Justin and Jacob returned to their area to find Lily rubbing her red cheek, and Karl sitting in a corner petting his cat.

Justin walked up to Lily.

"What happened to you?" asked Justin.

"It was that sister of his," Lily whispered in his ear. "She-"

"Attention all students," said a voice coming over the alien intercom. "We have discovered several potential planets which could be used to establish a colony. In a few moments, we shall attempt to use the alien's device to try and move faster than light. We have selected a planet we believe to be suitable for human life. That is all."

With anyone hardly noticing it, the black ship slipped into a starless pocket of space.

The ship was within a network of subspace fractures which allowed the vessel to bypass speed of light.

That night Denise prayed.

Lord, forgive me for slapping that girl, and help my brother to come out of his depression. Amen.

She concluded her prayers and tried to sleep.

Suddenly, she felt someone grab her legs.

She opened her eyes.

Two figures stood over her, but it was too dark for her recognize them.

Before Denise had a chance to react, she was bound and gagged.

She struggled to get free, but her efforts amounted to nothing as her captors were too strong.

She glanced over and saw a third figure grabbing what looked like a pair of shoes and some article of clothing.

"What are you doing?" asked the distorted voice of the figure holding her arms.

"No one would believe she started wandering around without her

37

pants or shoes," stated the distorted voice of the third figure. "Come on, let's get rid of her."

They carried her about a hundred feet from her group's area to an archway that led into a small chamber just large enough for the chair.

They tossed her in the chair and threw her shoes and pants on the floorboard in front of her.

One of the figures touched a panel on the side of the archway.

A door closed over the entrance and the small round pod was ejected into one of the red veins encircling the dark space corridor.

Lightening watched the final actions of the girls from the ventilation system.

While unable to affect Denise's immediate plight, the cat was sure he knew how to use the situation to accomplish his goal.

"We regret to inform you that second year student, Denise Sabers, is no longer with us." This shocking announcement came over the loudspeaker. "Based on the evidence, she somehow managed to launch herself out in one of the small life pods. With no way of finding her, we have no choice but to consider her lost."

Karl Sabers joined the rest of his group eating at a small table that was only a foot off the ground, as the message of his sister's demise reached them.

Karl put his food down and just sat there with a blank look.

"Well, can't say she'll be missed," Lily stated with a slightly cheerful tone in her voice. "Good riddance to bad rubbish."

"You shouldn't say things like that," said Brittany, looking rather depressed. "Denise was a friend of mine."

"Really," said Eva. "I didn't see you spend much time with her after the invasion."

"Let's end this, we've got work to do," said Justin. He put down his empty dish.

Karl ignored him.

Justin stood up and walked out of the room, followed by the others. Karl made no movement.

"Sabers, get going!"

"Forget it, he's too far gone," said Jacob.

The others walked off, leaving Karl in his daze. His yellow-orange long hair cat came out of his resting place and consumed Karl's meal, then turned and looked at Karl.

"Karl, you still there?" asked the cat.

"Family gone, home gone, sister gone," Karl stated with a monotone voice. "Work doesn't matter. Food doesn't matter. Life doesn't matter."

"Food doesn't matter?" asked the cat, with a puzzled expression on his face. "Guess I'm going to have to do some work here. Karl, look into my eyes."

"Look into your eyes," Karl said, looking down at the green eyes of the cat.

The young man and his cat sat there for several hours staring at each other without a sound, without movement, as though they were frozen in time. Karl finally blinked for a second.

"Lightening, what's going on?"

He raised his hand to his head and closed his eyes tightly as he felt a mind-splitting headache pass through his skull like a blade of ice.

At that point, Karl remembered everything that happened since the attack on the *Nomad*. There was almost no chance of seeing his parents again, and now his sister was gone. He had a vague understanding of how he had acted, up until this point, but it was as if he remembered someone else.

Like he had awakened from a nightmare.

"Lightening, what did you do?"

"That's not important right now," Lightening stated. "We have more pressing matters to deal with."

"And that is?" Karl asked, still rubbing his aching head.

"First, food," answered the cat. "Second, is getting your sister so that annoying distress signal will stop."

"What distress signal?" asked Karl.

"I forgot humans couldn't hear," said Lightening, licking his paws.

As it turned out, his sister's pod was sending off a signal broadcast through the intercom.

A sound that could not be heard by human ears.

Karl waited until the time that the Grand Council had designated as nighttime before hacking into the ship's systems. Somehow he was able to understand the series of colored geometric shapes which appeared on the screen in front of him.

As Lightening explained it, the Koal had implanted a translator device inside the head of each student. But most of the students were not yet aware of the device and, therefore, made no effort to read the alien language.

It was not long before Karl discovered three small attack vessels capable of traveling through the Dark Space Corridors.

Karl gathered his things, which included a few changes of clothing, his handheld computer, and his .45 automatic pistol.

He was quite pleased that the pistol and its three extra magazines had remained within the pockets of his Koal jacket during the time he was in his state of oblivion.

He then went down to the hangar deck, which hadn't been used at all by his fellow refugees.

He looked at the rows of catwalks all around him, which would be used to board the dozens of fighters and small attack crafts, found the flat triangular ship he needed. Using the panel in front of the vessel, he opened the small craft's lower hatch.

He suddenly heard footsteps coming down one of the catwalks above him.

Karl looked up and saw Justin and Jacob above him. The second they spotted Karl, he ran into the ship and hit the button to close the hatch. Justin and Jacob leaped from the catwalk and slid into the small attack vessel before the hatch closed shut.

"That was stupid," Lightening commented on Justin and Jacob's actions.

"Sabers, what are you doing?!" Justin demanded.

"I'm going to get my sister," Karl answered, pulling the .45 out of his coat. "I suggest you get off unless you want to come along for the ride."

"Sabers, you're not well," stated Jacob.

"Actually, I haven't felt this good in a long time," Karl said, walking over to the ship's helm, which consisted of several colored jewels that were used to control the operations of the vessel. He touched a red jewel and the ship jolted with the activation of her engines. "This is your last chance, get off, or tag along for the ride."

"Put down that antique," Justin said, trying to talk Karl out of leaving. "We need everyone to continue humanity on another planet."

"Your last chance," Karl warned them. "I'll gladly open the hatch and let you go."

"Please, there's no point in this. Listen to Justin," said Jacob.

The large doors of the hanger deck opened up and the small vessel flew out of the larger ship into the Dark Space Corridor.

As the three humans departed, Jacob and Justin stood there in shock. Neither one of them could believe what Karl had just done. They were now on a journey into the unknown.

Karl found the craft far easier to control than he previously believed. Following the signal through the black tunnels lined with red veins was like finding something in a video game. There was a map of corridors with an arrow pointing to the pod. All he had to do was make the turn where the corridors branched off.

The small ball shaped pod drifted across the starry blackness of space. The pod had reentered normal space when it struck one of the corridor's veins.

Denise had been too busy trying to get free to notice the red coating that vanished seconds after her pod exited dark space. After several hours, she finally managed to free her slender hands from its bindings. Then she freed herself from the gag and the bindings around her ankles.

They're going to pay for this, she thought to herself as she slipped her pants on. *When my brother comes to his senses and rescues me, I'm really going to make them pay. How should I best torture th-?*

"*Aurore* to escape pod," said a man's voice, which came from a panel near the chair. "This is the *Aurore*, do you read us?"

"Yes," Denise answered, without thinking.

"Good," said the voice. "We'll pick you up, hold tight."

She looked out of the round porthole of the pod and saw the black diamond shaped ship approaching her. Seeing no other option, she put her shoes on and waited to be picked up. She felt a jolt as the blue tractor beam pulled the pod into the *Aurore's cargohold.* The doors to the cargohold closed.

Several figures entered the cargohold. The bond between the hatch and the pod hissed as it separated. Standing in front of her when the hatch raised up was a red eyed man with metallic copper colored hair. There were at least five of these people who all had yellow, red, or purple eyes, and hair colored liked precious metals. She immediately realized that these were not ordinary humans.

"Girl, are you a citizen of either the Titan Empire or Mars Imperium?" asked the red eyed man.

"No," she answered. "I'm-" Within seconds, they all held curved pistol like objects that were pointed at her.

"Good, then you'll fetch a decent price on Darkfour," said the man with red eyes.

Two of the alien men grabbed her arms and started leading her down a brass corridor lined with glass columns. She stomped the foot of the man to her right and kneed the man to her left in the groin, then took off running. The alien on the right fired a blue shot from his pistol knocking Denise out cold.

In time, the signal led Karl to a star system with thirteen planets, five of which were rocky planets like Earth. A dark red coating covered the craft as they returned to normal space, peeling away within minutes. The small ship approached the planet where the signal was coming from, and to their surprise the planet was covered by a pink atmosphere.

As the ship drew closer to the system, the three of them saw spaceships of every shape and size appearing and disappearing all over the place. But that did not bother them nearly as much as seeing a pink planet.

A flashing symbol indicated someone was hailing the small vessel. Karl tapped a jewel which allowed the ship to receive communications.

A brown haired woman appeared on the main screen.

"Welcome to the Dainare system."

"She's human," Jacob stated in surprise.

"We are not responsible if your ship is lost or stolen, and we are not responsible if any of you is injured, killed, kidnapped, or sold into slavery. Have a nice day," said the woman, before her face vanished from the screen.

"Sounds like an inviting place," Karl said with a sarcastic tone.

"The human race looks like it survived just fine," Lightening said as Karl picked him up in his arms.

"Sabers, how do you know she didn't just look like a human?" stated Justin. "It could be some kind of trap set by the Koal."

Ignoring Justin, Karl flew the ship down through the pink bubblegum clouds and docked her in a hangar close to where the signal originated. He opened the port side hatch and entered into a hangar much like the one on the Koal mothership, filled with starships ranging from the size of a car, to larger than the *Nomad's* largest shuttles.

Followed by Lightening and the other two, he walked over to a lift which took them to a level with an actual floor.

Four men sat at a table playing cards. Two of the men got up and strode towards him. The older looking man and the other two men sitting at the table looked like Old Earth English Bobbie officers with dark blue capes. The other was a young man in his twenties.

Like Karl, he was wearing a Koal jacket, but his was old, faded, and the triangular buckles were tarnished. On his right hip he had a revolver with an ivory handle, and on his left he had a Japanese katana with a dragon hilt. The young man looked just like a normal human except for his metallic copper colored hair.

"You there," the older man said to Karl. "I need to know your name, the name of that ship, and the registry."

"Karl Sabers, and this is my cat, Lightening," he answered. "As for the name of my ship…"

He paused while trying to think of a name for the vessel.

"How about the *Devil's Fang*?" Justin said, as an insult.

"*Devil's Fang* registered to a Mr. Karl Sabers," said the older man. "Now, for the docking fee."

Karl quickly realized he had nothing that he could use as currency.

"That coat will cover the price for about three days."

"A coat like that would cover the docking fees for at least a month and a half," said the copper haired man, with a smirk on his face.

The older man glared at the younger man, as Karl handed him the Koal jacket. "Well, you can have your ship docked here for a month and a half." The older man reluctantly stated. "Well, that will be all. I hope you enjoy your stay on Dainare III."

"You probably won't," said the copper haired man, as he waved to the other three men. "Watch your step around here. Pirates and crimps all over the place."

"Thanks," Karl said, turning to Lightening. "Let's go." Karl started tracking the signal from the escape pod on his handheld.

As they walked down the street, Karl looked up at the sky and saw that it was also pink. "That is really starting to bother me."

"I really don't see why you have a problem with that color," Lightening said.

"It's a human guy thing," Karl answered.

"I like the color," said Justin.

"Same here," Jacob stated. Karl slowly moved away from the two.

"When do we eat?" Lightening asked.

Just as Karl was about to answer, he saw three black helmets, each with a single spike, moving through a crowd of people.

"Koal!"

He drew his .45 pistol.

As the three armored Koal moved closer, the four searchers ran into a nearby shop. Once they were inside, he put away his weapon.

"I wonder why they're here?"

"Looking for something to eat." Lightening licked his tail. "When do we eat?"

"I know how you feel." Karl's stomach rumbled. "I'm hungry too." Then Karl heard a beeping noise. He looked at his handheld and soon realized the pod was somewhere within the area of the shop.

Footsteps behind brought them to attention. "What are you doing here?" a male voice said. They turned to see an old man with a white mustache.

The man was dressed in a frock coat with a red waistcoat, wearing a pair of black gloves. In his right hand was a wooden cane with a dragon head.

"The store is closed."

"I'm sorry, but your door was open," Karl answered.

"Well." The old man pulled a round object from his jacket. It was about the size and shape of a hockey puck. He placed his thumb on the glass center of the object and an orange ring lit up around it. "Isabel, get down here!"

A young blonde haired girl ran down a set of stairs. The man turned towards the girl, whose ears were pointed and covered in thin gray fur. "You left the door open. That means I'll be cutting the lead content of your food to pay for any merchandise that was stolen because of your carelessness."

"I'm sorry, master," she apologized. "It won't happen again!"

Lead? Karl thought to himself. *Does this girl want this old man to poison her?*

"It better not," said the man.

As the girl left, the visitors noticed a gray wolf like tail coming out from underneath her coat.

The man turned back to Karl. "And now for you."

"Goodbye," Lightening said.

He and Karl started towards the door. Then everything outside the

45

door turned to a pale shade of blue.

"All right, what can I do you for?" he asked, reaching into his vest pocket to pull out a pair of glasses. He wiped his glasses and put them on his face.

"Lunch," Lightening answered.

Karl stood there. "I thought you were closed," he said, as Lightening rubbed against his legs.

"I think I can handle a few more customers," the old man said, putting the object back in his jacket. "Is there something you're interested in?"

"Yes," Karl said, as he picked up Lightening. "I'm looking for an escape pod that might have ended up here a short time ago."

"Sabers, what are you doing?" Jacob asked.

"I think my sister's pod is in this shop," Karl whispered to the others.

"You should ask him what his name is," Lightening whispered, in Karl's ear just before biting his neck.

"Ow. What's your name?" Karl asked.

"Ashley Claymore. And by the way, I did come by an old Lecaran escape pod last week," he stated, scratching his head. "Would you like to see it?"

A week. That was far too long. Denise had only been missing for a little over a day and a half. "Is there a pod that would have been brought in sometime later?" Karl asked. "Like within the last twenty-four hours?"

"Master!" said the wolf girl, with a smile on her face as she returned to the old man's side. "I have confirmed that nothing was stolen." The three Earth men stared at the girl as her furry tail wagged like the tail of a dog. "So that means I won't be punished, right?"

"If nothing was stolen, I'll let you off the hook this time," said Ashley.

"And I did some research on that pod you bought from that freighter captain yesterday," she stated. "The idiot didn't know what he had. It's from the same class of ships that attacked Old Earth. It's worth fifty times the 40,000 Titan Cronos you paid for it."

"Well, come on," said Claymore, with a smirk on his face. "I don't plan to wait around here. The pod Isabel mentioned may be the one you are looking for."

46

The three humans started following the old man. "Lightening, do you think it's a good idea to be following him like this?" asked Karl, as Lightening jumped out of his arms.

"Don't worry, I'll protect you," Lightening said, as they walked through the rows of strange looking junk. "As long as I'm fed."

Karl and Lightening followed Claymore into an elevator that had no buttons or levers of any kind, leaving Justin and Jacob on the upper level with Isabel watching them.

The door closed and then opened a few seconds later into a hangar. The hangar was smaller than the one they had landed in earlier, but the ships in this place were much more impressive than ones Karl had seen in the system.

The largest ship resembled Earth's World War I type German U-boat. It had two rings, one on each side of the ship. Beside it was a gold saucer, which looked like it came right out of a 1950s science fiction movie.

The most interesting of all were the fighters above them. There were about forty of them. Each of them had a long hexagon shaped fuselage with a crescent wing on top of the fighter.

"There they are," Claymore said, pointing to two objects. The first looked like a triangular pyramid the size of a bus, the other was a round black ball just large enough for a single person to climb inside.

Karl had Lightening investigate. The cat sniffed. He confirmed that the pod was indeed the one in which Denise had been launched.

"Where did you get it?" Karl asked, wondering what might have happened to his sister.

"The Lecaran captain of a cargo vessel sold it to me," Ashley answered. "He claimed that he found the thing abandoned in space. It wasn't my place to argue and it was a cheap price."

"You wouldn't happen to know the name of the captain and where his ship was headed?" asked Karl, as he scratched Lightening's back.

"I can't remember his name off hand, but I do remember his ship was the *Aurore* and he was headed for Darkfour."

"Lecaran?" Karl inquired. "Are they some other type of alien?"

Claymore chuckled in reaction to Karl's comment. "I see your people must've left Earth during the invasion," Claymore stated. "Your lack of knowledge of the Lecarans and the way you dress give it away. You're from one of the lost colony ships that disappeared into

47

the void of space."

Karl backed up, a look of panic on his face. *He knows where I am from.*

"Relax that's something that we have in common. Like you, my people were also launched into space and remained adrift until we arrived, only to find our destination had already been colonized by the Martian Imperium."

"So what ship are you from?" asked Karl.

"That part is not something I talk about." Claymore sighed and removed his glasses.

"Now, who are the Lecarans?" Karl asked, figuring that the Lecarans were the aliens who had his sister.

"We can talk all about them later. On to lunch." Claymore strolled towards the elevator.

Lunch? I could like this guy, Lightening thought.

Karl walked behind Claymore. Lightening followed close.

"I have a friend that I'm meeting with. Now, you need to change into something that won't draw much attention."

Karl left the shop wearing a brown three piece suit and a fedora. At first it felt strange to be wearing clothes that looked so old fashioned, but he soon realized that nearly everyone around them wore frock coats with hats. Even Jacob and Justin were forced to dress in this style.

The four humans and the cat stepped into what looked like an old motorcar from the early twentieth century.

The only difference in appearance was that the wheels were flat on the ground. The wheels started spinning and the car lifted off the ground, then began moving to its destination.

The ride came to an end when the car landed in front of a western looking saloon.

They entered the saloon, which was empty except for a robotic bartender.

Is this a museum?

Karl thought it was a bit strange that there was no one there.

Why does this place seem like an ancient cowboy bar?

Before he could really think about anything else, the image before him turned to static and everything went black.

48

Chapter 8- Shanghaied

"Get up."

Karl felt something hard hit him in the stomach. With his right hand on his stomach, he got to his knees. He opened his eyes and felt a throbbing pain in the back of his head. Karl placed his left hand on the back of his head and felt something dry and crusty in his hair. He pulled back his hand and looked down at the brown flecks of dried blood in his hand.

Slowly he got to his feet. Jacob and Justin were standing next to him. Looking directly at him was a large human of Ancient Zulu descent. He was dressed in a black jumpsuit and had an object which looked like a policeman's club, only this was silver and had three small blue gems on top. He did not look like a man with gigantism but about like an average person. It was only when Karl stood next to him he could tell the man would have been a giant on the *Nomad*.

Karl looked around the room, which was gray and rather plain. It could have been mistaken for a prison cell, but the large metal and plastic crates showed that it was a storage room or a cargohold. Something that struck Karl as being rather odd was the size and shape of most of the crates in the room. The containers reminded him a lot of coffins, and each of them had a glowing green panel on it. But before he could even consider examining them, the tall man forced them down a narrow hallway with gray metal walls until they reached a metal door with a large crank.

"Pope John Paul XVI is once again on Martian soil," Karl heard from beyond the door. "His Holiness was welcomed back to New Vatican City following his visit to the ruins of St. Peter's Basilica."

They still have popes? Karl thought, as he waited for what was beyond the door. *I wonder what else survived the fall of Earth.*

The man turned the crank and they entered an office. At a metal desk was a man of Asian descent wearing a white long-sleeved shirt and a brown waistcoat. He stood up, revealing his height of about six feet and walked over to the three men. He circled around the three of them five times and examined each of them carefully.

This made Karl feel very uncomfortable.

How am I going to escape from this? Karl knew his .45 automatic had likely been taken, and there was no way he could take down the big guy. Even if the three of them got together and brought him down, the other man was most likely armed with a weapon of some kind.

"Allow me to introduce myself," said the Asian man. "I am Captain Ling, captain of the *Starlight*. As members of the *Starlight's* crew, you shall receive the salary of 60,000 Titan Cronos a month and..."

"Excuse me, but we are not part of your crew so I think we need to be going," Justin stated. The gems on the larger man's club started glowing blue. The man with the club walked over to Justin and jabbed him in the stomach with the club. Justin fell to the ground, a jolt of electricity ran through him.

The captain held up a round device similar to the one Claymore had.

"According to this, you have a six months contract as a crew member aboard this ship," he said, as a holographic window with the names and pictures of each of them appeared above the object. "Telmak, show these men to their quarters."

"Aye, aye, Captain," answered the larger man.

Telmak forced the three men down a long narrow corridor. Along the hallway were doors, each of which was two feet wide and four feet apart. They stopped at a door labeled 'cabin number 20'. The door slid apart revealing a small empty room which was only six feet wide and eight feet long. The only visible object in the room was a silver panel on the back wall of the cabin.

"You shall receive you orders momentarily," said Telmak. "The panel controls the objects in the room." Telmak left them in their cabin.

They went to the metal panel. Justin stretched out his hand and touched it. Then a hologram monitor and keyboard appeared in front of them. It worked about like a computer from the *Nomad*, but this one was far more advanced, to the point that they could even feel the keys on the holographic keyboard.

Karl reached in his pocket and found one of the handheld computers like the one Claymore and the captain had. Once he activated the object, the image of Claymore's head and shoulders appeared in front of him.

"Don't tell Justin and Jacob that I am talking to you," said the image of Claymore. "Well, Mr. Sabers, I have good news and bad news for you. The good news is, the person you're looking for is probably on Darkfour and you may be able to see them soon. And the bad news is that if your friend is there, you'll have to buy that person's freedom. So out of the kindness of my heart I have taken the liberty of providing you a job. So all you'll have to do is wait a month for the person to appear on the market as an indentured servant. While you're waiting, you can earn the money to pay for your friend. It should only cost you half of your first paycheck." The image faded and Karl hit a button to activate a bunk. The bed slid out of the wall and he sat down. "Oh, and you can pay for the handheld next time you come to my shop."

"I'm never going back to that place," Karl yelled at the handheld as Justin and Jacob covered their ears. "You son of a b-"

"MEOW." Lightening let his presence be known.

Denise found herself in a large room with no windows or doors. The only light came from a set of panels on the ceiling, suspended at least thirty feet in the air.

Denise stood up.

She soon noticed that she was not the only person in the room. On the floor nearby were three other women. One had long brown hair and wore a tuxedo. Another was a blonde woman in a pink dress. The last was a black haired woman in a blood red military uniform.

The woman in the red uniform walked over to Denise.

"Hello there," she said, staring at Denise with her dark blue eyes. "What are you supposed to be?"

"Huh?" the woman's question confused her a little.

The woman pointed at Denise's pirate costume which she had been wearing since the raid on the *Nomad*. "So, what are you in for?" she asked.

"I haven't done anything," Denise answered. "What am I doing here?"

"That's what they all say," said the woman with a chuckle. "But it is true that sometimes people are brought to this place on false charges. Tell me did the people who brought you here have metallic hair?"

"Yes," answered Denise.

"Then it was the Lecarans," said the woman.

"Lecarans?" she asked. "Do they have something to do with the Ruby Eyed Empress?"

"Let me guess, you're from a planet which has almost no dealing with events off world," she stated, getting Denise's situation more right than she realized. "I'm right, aren't I?"

Denise nodded her head.

"Well then, I'll tell you. While they claim themselves to be as natural as our kind, the Lecarans are a race of yellow blooded aliens that were altered to create a cheap imitation of the Terran species. After nature had forced them off the world they occupied, they sent the Koal to invade Earth in their jealousy. The Earth rejected them, so they sold the Earth to another race. Even after a thousand years, a thorn in the side of Terrans."

"What is this place?!" Denise asked, becoming frantic on the inside. "Some type of prison?!"

"Well, you could say that," said the woman. "But it would more accurate to call this place a processing plant."

"What kind of processing plant?" Denise asked with a worried tone in her voice.

"Well, this place is commonly used to convert criminals into indentured servants," said the dark haired woman. "What happens is, when a person commits a crime they are given the option of serving their sentence in a prison, or a worker camp, or coming here. Most people prefer to come here."

"And what do they actually do to us here?" Denise asked, calming herself down by trying to remember that this was all a test of faith.

"They're going to implant skills that the average person would find useful," she answered. "Then they put on a silver bracelet that will only come off when your sentence is up. After that, you'll be bought and your memories will be sealed until the bracelet comes off and if the bracelet is removed prematurely, your memories will be gone forever."

Denise really felt like she was going to freak out.

"Oh, I haven't introduced myself yet. I'm Helena Anders, Supreme Commander of Blood Terra, and my organization has a way of helping you, if you're interested."

Denise felt a sudden jolt and noticed the ceiling was getting

52

closer. She realized that the entire floor was a gigantic elevator. It stopped about ten feet from the ceiling, the wall on her left slid away. Twelve men in gray uniforms stood, waiting for them.

Each of the girls was grabbed by two men. Denise tried to fight them off, but something cold touched the back of her neck making her body go limp. Denise awoke to find herself strapped to a metal chair.

"You have been found guilty of piracy in the third degree and are hereby sentenced to five years as an indentured servant," said a man in a gray uniform.

A man in a white lab coat walked over to Denise. In his hand was a small glass cylinder filled glowing green liquid, with a piece of metal on the end.

He held it up before her.

She tried to cry out, but no words came. The man placed the metal piece on her neck.

Denise felt a shock, then passed out.

She awoke to find herself back in the cell with other girls. Denise saw Helena walking towards her.

"You better get used to it. They are going to do that process six more times over the next month."

A month had passed since the refugees from the *Nomad* had come aboard the cargo ship. Each of them had been given jobs on the ship. Jacob and Justin's duties consisted primarily of serving the crew meals and cleaning up.

Karl, on the other hand, had spent his time learning about the ship's systems, and within two weeks he had been assigned to work with the ship's mechanic.

Over the past month, Karl had managed to locate his sister and had discovered that she had been sentenced to five years of servitude. He was ready with the money he had earned working on the ship. He was going to try to place an order to purchase his sister on a subspace version of the internet.

Karl sat down on the bunk. He hit a button on the panel which made a small table rise up from the floor. He placed his computer on the surface of the table.

"If you're going to order food," said the cat. The transparent image of a screen and keyboard appeared. "I'll take some roast beef with a side of bacon."

"Lightening, I'm not ordering food," Karl said, as he scrolled through the list of women on the site.

"No, you're just buying female companions online," Lightening said, jumping on the bed beside Karl. "Which is far less interesting."

"That makes it sound like I'm doing something dirty," Karl stated as he came to his sister's page. She had a 50,000 credit tag on her. The description read-

Species- Terran.
Condition- good, no handling.
Eyes- green.
Hair- brown.
Skin- light brown.
Blood Type- B Negative.
Skills- cooking, cleaning, and drawing.
Current Status- SOLD, Indentured servant five years sentence.

Well, that's just perfect, Karl thought to himself, placing his right hand on his forehead. "What do I do now?" he said out loud.

"Have lunch and wait five years for her to regain her freedom," said the cat.

"Guess I could try tracking down her master," he said, waving his hand causing the screen to vanish. *Have to get off this ship first.*

"This is the captain speaking," said a voice from the ship intercom. "We will be in the Tau Ceti system within the hour. All crew are to report to their stations."

Karl departed from his cabin and made his way down the corridor to the engine room. Standing on a catwalk in the engine room, overlooking the ship's reactor, was the mechanic of the vessel, Alice. The slender dark skinned girl, like Telmak, was from the moons of Jupiter and was slightly taller than Karl. She may have been only sixteen years old, but Alice was brilliant when it came to understanding the workings of faster than light ships.

"Prepare for a flash point," she stated, just before the whole ship lit up with a white light, and then quickly returned to its normal form.

"So, Alice," he said. "What would happen if a man was to jump ship?"

"Sabers, if you jump ship, the captain will send a bounty hunter to bring you back," she answered. "And if a bounty hunter brings you back, you will have to work twice as long without any pay."

"Well, I guess we can give up on that plan," Karl whispered under his breath, turning his head to peer up at an air vent. "What do you think, Lightening?"

"It will work, so long as you don't get caught," Lightening answered.

"That is easier said than done," Karl said to the cat.

An object, the size and shape of a baseball, dropped from the ceiling and hovered in the center of the room.

"Attention all crew, this is the captain speaking." The captain's voice came from the sphere. "All crew will report to the cargo deck and begin transport of freight."

As ordered, Karl made his way to the cargohold and took part in the transport of the coffin-like boxes. Each was placed on a trolley and moved out of the cargohold through the narrow corridors of the ship. Once the majority of containers were removed from the cargohold, Karl saw only one remaining. This one was covered with a thin layer of dust. Karl tentatively examined the crate. It looked almost undisturbed as if it had been left in a tomb.

"Hey, what about this one?" Karl asked, looking to see if there were was still room on the trolley for the last container. But there was no one there.

As Karl turned to leave, his foot tapped a green panel on the side of the container. The panel turned red. With a loud clank, the container's lid lifted up an inch. White cold air spilled out of the gap. The cover split down the middle and slid down each side.

Karl had never known what the cargo actually was, but he had entertained a suspicion, which he had tried to push to the back of his mind.

This confirmed it.

Inside the container was a girl.

The *Starlight* was a slave ship.

And they had just transported a cargo consisting of slaves, most likely destined to be auctioned.

The beautiful young woman in her late teens had long metallic gold hair. She was dressed in a silver halter top and short silver skirt.

She looked like she was sleeping peacefully, with her hands coming together over her stomach.

Embedded in her right wrist was a gold bracelet.

On the upper part of her left arm was a silver band with long thin triangular spikes coming from both sides, flat along her arm.

On her feet glittered a pair of high heels that looked like they were made of frosted glass.

The girl's hands began to move apart and she slowly rose up. She turned her head towards Karl and raised her eyelids revealing her ruby red irises. She placed her left hand on the side of the container.

"Well, Mr. Sabers."

Karl turned to see the figure of the captain standing behind him.

"I hope you're planning on paying for that. This one will be coming out of your paycheck."

"What is that girl doing in this container?" Karl asked, still staring at the girl.

"About a year ago this stasis pod showed up with another shipment," the captain answered. "I tried to contact the supplier, but he had no record of this one. I didn't want to risk getting the girl out of stasis to have her listed, and then not be able to get her back in when I was done. But now that you're here, she's your problem," he smirked. "Unless you plan on being arrested."

"Damn!" Karl stated. He pulled out his handheld and watched as the number 60,000 appeared on the computer, and then went down to 39,000. Once the transaction was complete, the captain departed leaving Karl and the girl behind. "Great, 21,000 credits down the drain."

"Well, Karl." Lightening said, with a lick of his fur. "Looks like you bought yourself a girl."

Karl took the girl's cold right hand to help her out of the container. Karl noticed a less striking feature compared to her red eyes, just as his knuckles and fingertips were red or pinkish in appearance, hers were a very pale yellow. As the girl stepped out of the container, Karl took notice of a gold rod housed in a small pocket on the side of the container. The object had a blue crystal on one end and a strange series of buttons on the other. He picked up the object and stuffed it into his vest pocket.

"So, what's your name?" asked Karl, looking into the girl's alien eyes.

"I'm a slave," she answered. "I don't have a name. My number is LG0495238. My first memories are of you standing over my stasis pod," she answered. "My memories were sealed after the last time I was sold."

"We'll have to work on a name," Karl stated.

"I hear Whiskers and Fluffy are popular," Lightening suggested.

Karl and Lightening returned to their cabin with the girl. As they made their way down the corridor, Karl glanced over at the girl's glass shoes.

How is she able to walk in those? Karl thought to himself as the door slid open to his cabin. To his surprise, Justin and Jacob were already gone. *At least I don't have to explain anything to them right now.*

"What am I going to do with her?" Karl asked, aloud without realizing it.

"Well, if you make starship captain this'll seem perfectly reasonable," Lightening stated as he jumped onto one of the bunks.

"I doubt that you'll be able to get your money back," said the alien girl. "There's not much of a market for cyborgs." The girl pointed to the metal band on her left arm. "Most people aren't going to want me once they have to deal with paying for the upkeep of a prosthetic."

Now she's a cyborg alien slave girl, Karl thought, closing his eyes in disbelief.

"And next thing you know she'll be a princess," Lightening commented, licking his tail.

"Both of you out," Karl demanded. *I hope shore leave is less stressful.*

A few moments later Karl stepped out of his cabin wearing a long-sleeved shirt and a waistcoat. The slave girl immediately ran back into his room and grabbed a jacket and a fedora, then handed them to Karl. "You look like a barbarian if you're only half dressed," she stated, handing him his outer garments.

Reluctantly Karl slipped on the coat and hat before they departed the ship. As the three of them left, he saw the outside of the ship for the first time. She was shaped like a long rectangular box with a rocket on each of the back corners.

"What a lame looking ship," Lightening stated. As they departed the ship, the figure of a man with metallic copper hair and dressed in a black coat made his way beyond them.

"Yeah, I know. And I still have five months aboard that thing," Karl said to his feline friend.

Unlike Dainare III, this planet looked more like Earth did in history before the fall.

However, the towers were too small to be tower cities like those of Old Earth. And this world had a large number of flying vehicles which were moving on transparent red streets.

They walked over to a taxi, which was yellow and black and looked like a huge horizontal egg, with two parallel rods on each side of it.

They made themselves comfortable in the back seat. Lightening clutching Karl's neck and the girl beside him.

"Nearest shopping mall," Karl directed the driver.

Without a glance back from the front seat occupant, the cab started up and gained height, flying slow.

"So, besides not having a name, could you tell me anything else about yourself?"

"I told you. My first memories are of you standing over my stasis pod. My memories were sealed after the last time I was sold. All I know is that I am a Lecaran slave and a cheap one at that. The Neith Empire would be the most likely place of origin for me because nearly all the aristocracy was forced into slavery after the Revolution, which greatly expanded the number of slaves on the market."

Karl felt sympathy for the girl, but he still had no idea what to do about her.

Freeing her was not much of an option since she had nowhere to go.

Plus, he had already invested a good bit of money in her and he didn't want to see that go to waste.

Lightening climbed off Karl's shoulder and into the girl's lap.

She placed her right hand on the cat and started petting him.

"Karl, it's time to eat," Lightening said, purring away in the girl's arms.

Despite the fact that he felt sorry for her, he felt a little jealous that she was giving the cat attention. He looked out the window and saw an advertisement for a restaurant named *Lady Sophia,* which was built into the same tower as a clothing store. Karl ordered the driver to park in front of the tower. He wanted something to eat and the girl needed something else to wear.

Lightening and Karl spent the next six hours waiting, as the alien girl tried on hundreds of outfits to find a few things she liked. It only took Karl less than an hour to buy a few more suits, which he thought made him appear more presentable among the civilians of the Galaxy. Having completed his purchases, he had nothing better to do than sit there and pet his cat.

"What do you think about this?" asked the Lecaran girl. She came out of the dressing room in a black jacket with a knee length skirt and blood red blouse.

"You look very good," he answered. "Sophia." He looked at the girl and smiled.

"Huh?" asked the girl.

"What do you think of the name Sophia?" he asked, as Lightening started taking a bath in the middle of the store.

"For what," she replied, trying to sound as polite as possible. "May I ask?"

"Yourself, of course," he answered. "I can't possibly remember LG48... whatever the rest of it was."

"LG0495238," she corrected him.

She gasped, realizing that correcting her master could be taken as a sign of rebellion. "I'm sorry. I didn't mean to- I was only-" She shut her eyes and clenched her teeth.

"What's wrong?" he asked. "I'm not going hurt you or anything."

She slowly opened her eyes again. "You're not going to use the control rod on me?" asked the girl.

Karl had a bit of a confused look on his face. "Are you talking about this gold rod?" he asked as he pulled the rod out of his jacket. "I thought it was a receipt or something."

"So, you don't have any idea how to use that thing do you?" she stated. "Well then, may I see it? I might be able to access some information about my past with that." He handed her the device and she darted by him, running from the women's section.

"You should have expected that," Lightening said, licking his paws.

"How far can she get in heels?" Karl said, with a smirk on his face. "Also, I haven't paid for her clothes yet, so the cops will be onto her soon."

"She's a slave," said the cat. "They may just kill her and save themselves the trouble of catching her."

Lightening had a point. And she was also a Lecaran, which made the situation even worse.

"Lightening, cut her off," he said, taking off after her.

Karl chased her through the men's clothes. He had a hard time keeping up with the girl as she zigzagged through the clothing racks.

Surprisingly, she ran very well for someone wearing high heels. She managed to get to the checkout area before Karl had a chance to see her get by the men's section.

Between her and the door was the dark skinned girl, Alice, dressed in a three piece suit not too different Karl's.

Sophia tripped over Lightening and landed on Alice, losing her control rod.

When Karl got there, he found the alien girl on top of Alice.

He picked up the rod.

Lightening was busy giving himself another bath.

"A little too chaotic for my taste," he said to the cat.

"It's not my fault that she didn't have sense enough to bend over and pet me," Lightening replied. "Plus, you told me to cut her off. Time for you to feed me now."

"Get off me! Whose slave is this?" Alice demanded after seeing the slave bracelet on the Lecaran's arm.

Because Alice appeared of African descent and remembering 19th century US history, Karl was hesitant to admit that he was a slave owner. "That would be me," Karl reluctantly stated as the two girls stood up.

"Oh!" Alice said in a semi-surprised voice. "You need to keep better control over your slave. If she doesn't behave herself, you could be charged with any crime that she commits."

"You're not at all bothered by the fact that I own a slave?" Karl asked, being semi-disturbed over the ease at which Alice accepted the situation.

"What? Slavery has been legal since the invasion of Earth," she said, picking up her bags. "The problem is that you bought a female alien. Now everyone is going to know about your Xenofetish." Alice stared at the girl for a few moments, before turning back "Karl, I didn't think you owned a slave."

"I sort of ended up with her by accident," Karl replied.

"Is that the one that the captain's been trying to get rid of for the last couple of years?" asked Alice. "I thought the captain had already found a buyer for her. I don't see why she's stuck with you."

Alice then left Karl with the alien girl to continue shopping on her own.

After their run-in with Alice, Karl paid for the clothes and they went to the *Lady Sophia* restaurant, which Karl's new slave was named after.

Luckily the place catered to both the brown and blue eyed Terran as well as the red and yellow eyed Lecaran. Separate menus were given for the two races, because Lecaran food was seasoned with things that would be poisonous to Terrans. Lead, mercury, and cyanide to name a few.

Karl was rather disappointed that the only utensil he was given to eat with was a double edged knife. Karl's meal consisted of some kind of crab-like thing, and Lightening claimed one of its ten legs. Sophia ate something that looked like a noodle soup with a black broth.

The meal was uncomfortably quiet. Sophia had given up almost any hope of escaping and remained silent through the entire meal.

In addition, Karl did not have any idea of what he should say. He leaned back and glanced over towards three men that were having a drink together.

Two were Lecaran, the younger one had metallic silver hair and the other was an older looking man whose metallic gold hair was blackening with age. The third was a Terran that Karl was already familiar with.

Ashley Claymore rose from his seat and made his way over to Karl and the alien.

"Well, boy, it looks like we meet again," said Claymore, with a smile on his face. "Looks like you've done all right for yourself."

"You," Karl said, glaring back at him. "Knocked me out, robbed me and dumped me on a random cargo ship."

"Come now," Claymore stated with a slight smile, "there was nothing random about the *Starlight.* Besides you needed a job to pay for that sister of yours, and I'm sorry to hear that things did not work out with getting her back."

Everything Claymore said did nothing except further enrage Karl to the point he was ready to grab his pistol and gun him down.

His right hand slid towards the hilt of his weapon, but his left hand rose up and grabbed his wrist holding his fingers back from the gun's black handle.

"Now we can get down to business." Ashley turned his gaze towards Sophia. "You seemed to have acquired the package I was planning on picking up later. Now if you would be so kind as to hand her over."

"Why? I paid for her." Karl stepped in front of Sophia.

"Of course, there's your delivery payment, which would be about 30,000 credits," Ashley replied.

"I think she's worth much more that," Karl stated, his glare at the old man slowly turned to a smirk.

While Karl was occupied, Lightening hopped on the table and started eating off Karl's plate.

"First there's the cost of buying her, then there's the cost of her clothes, and this meal came to about 950 credits. Sophia, how much would the combined cost be?"

"That's about 45,000," she stated.

"And a third of that you spent on yourself," Lightening whispered.

Karl turned back towards the cat. "So to make a profit I would need more than 45,000," Karl whispered back to the feline.

Claymore chuckled. "I guess she's your problem for the moment." He turned and went back to his two friends leaving Karl and Sophia behind with the cat.

When Karl and Sophia finished eating, they went back outside and motioned to another cab which slid over towards them. Lightening and the girl followed Karl as he got in the taxi.

The taxi took off. She stared out the window and not a word slipped out of her yellow lips.

As they rode on, Karl noticed the road suddenly change from the transparent red streets to metal. The taxi veered into a dark alley and stopped. The driver got out and walked over to a man in a black coat standing in the shadows.

Then the driver returned, opened the door next to the girl, grabbed her wrist and jerked her out of the taxi. He dragged her over to the man in the black coat.

Karl pulled his gun out and exited the vehicle.

He pointed the weapon.

"Let her go!" Karl demanded. He had paid good money for this girl and he wasn't about to let someone just take her, especially since she was attractive.

The taxi driver turned his head towards Karl. "Walk away, boy," said the driver. "This doesn't co-"

In the right hand of the other man was a sickle sword. With a swift action, the glass blade was slashed through the taxi driver.

The body dropped to the ground.

"Stupid Earthling, you should blame that stupid cargo ship captain for not selling me the girl when I first made my offer." The killer came from the shadows into the light.

Karl could now see the man in the black coat clearly.

He was a Lecaran with dark yellow eyes, and long metallic copper hair which went below his shoulders.

"Now, for you." He pointed his weapon at Karl.

"Why does this keep happening?" Karl aimed his gun at the yellow eyed man.

With his left hand, the man pulled a black sphere similar to the ones used by the Koal to disable weapons onboard the *Nomad*.

"Have you found a way to stop gunpowder from burning?" Karl asked, with a smirk on his face.

"What's 'gunpowder'?" asked the man.

Karl squeezed the trigger and fired at the man. However, his feeling of victory quickly turned to despair as Karl watched the bullets shatter inches before reaching his enemy's chest.

The glass khopesh sword in the Lecaran man's hand glowed orange as he drew closer to Karl.

Before Karl had a chance to contemplate his next course of action, Lightening gripped onto the yellow eyed man's arm.

"AHAAA!" the alien screamed, as the claws of the yellow-orange tabby sank into his flesh.

The alien grabbed the long hair cat by the neck, tearing Lightening from his arm and throwing the feline to the floor. A dark yellow liquid dripped from the gashes left by the cat. "You'll pay for that, Terran!" Casting aside his sword, the yellow eyed man pulled a black rod with a glowing red gem from his coat.

Karl heard a loud crash behind. He turned and saw a black metal skeleton with no eye sockets standing six feet in front of him.

On each of the skeleton's wrists was a long thin black blade that ran along the arm. The blade on its right arm swung out 180 degrees, and the mechanical skeleton ran at Karl.

He opened fire, but bullets had no effect on its metal body. He jumped to his right, dodging the first swing.

With Karl distracted by the robot, the copper haired man smacked the girl in the face, knocking her to the ground, then drew a large black dagger with his uninjured left hand.

As she tried to raise herself from the ground, the black blade came at her, and she blocked it with her left arm. The dagger cut through the synthetic flesh covering her mechanical wrist.

She grabbed the sword from the ground beside her and slashed open the stomach of the alien man.

"Karl!" the girl yelled, sliding the glass sword towards Karl. "That blade has a charge-cutter."

The skeleton turned and swung at him again.

Karl dropped his gun and blocked the skeleton's blade with the sickle sword. He blocked three more swings before the skeleton released its second blade.

"Charge what?!" Karl yelled, as he blocked another blow.

He then noticed a ring just above where the grip of the sickle sword met the top of the knuckle guard. Squeezing the ring like a trigger caused the glass blade in his hand to glow orange.

The skeleton swung with its right arm at him again, but this time instead of blocking the black blade, the glowing blade sliced right through it. He slashed at the skeleton's right leg and severed it.

As the robotic frame crashed to the ground, Karl swung his sword and decapitated it.

Karl turned to face his opponent. Instead he saw the alien face down in a puddle of dark yellow liquid.

The ruby eyed girl had already cut down the would-be murderer before giving the alien weapon to Karl.

Chapter 9- The Bounty Hunter

Karl and Sophia climbed into the hover taxi. Karl pulled a rag from his jacket pocket and handed it to the gold haired girl.

She wiped away the dark yellow liquid from her mouth, which Karl then realized was her alien blood.

The assassin was the first alien which had died after an encounter with Karl since the battle at the Academy.

"What are we going to do now?" Karl asked, looking at Sophia.

On the *Nomad*, the course of action would have been to contact the police and plead self-defense. But Karl had no way of contacting what counted as a police force on this planet.

"Can't we get away?" asked Sophia.

"I cannot drive this thing."

"You mean you can drive Koal ships but not taxicabs?"

"It's a stick shift."

"You expect me to get you out of this mess, don't you? I don't think you would approve of how we felines take care of our kills," Lightening stated. "The human thing to do would be to dump bodies in the trunk and leave 'em here while we get off this world."

"Surely leaving the bodies behind leaves us to become suspects in a murder investigation," said Karl Sabers.

"Don't let that concern yourself," said the all too unpleasant voice of Ashley Claymore from the handheld in Karl's pocket.

A few moments later, a dark blue floating transport pulled up beside them. The side hatch of the vehicle opened and Claymore exited. Beside him were the two alien men that he had been dining with earlier.

"Congratulations, you've done far better than I expected!" Claymore exclaimed at Karl.

Karl pointed his new sword at the old man. "You followed us!"

"I'm afraid the two of you are too valuable to leave unattended," Claymore stated with a smirk.

"I appreciate the compliment, although I do not know why you are including the slave girl, as I am clearly more valuable than anyone anywhere around here." The long hair tabby cat swiped his ear with his paw.

Claymore looked at the cat.

"While the slave girl is marginal, I do find Karl to be worth a lot, so don't discount him," Lightening further commented, wiping his face. "He's my source of cat food."

Claymore shook himself and turned away from the cat.

"You'll have to come with us," Claymore stated to Karl and Sophia while glancing back at the two aliens. "Calidi, Ellris, grab them, without any unnecessary injuries."

Karl raised his new sword. He squeezed the trigger and the blade glowed orange.

Calidi and Ellris were just standing in the same place looking at each other. Ellris ran his hand through his silver hair. Calidi shook his head, then ran his finger along his nose. Ellris nodded. From behind their jackets, they both pulled retractable handled halberds with glass axe blades and top-mounted spearheads.

The handles extended out three feet and the two alien men began circling Karl, as the blade in the hand of Ellris became yellow and the weapon in the hand of Calidi became red. Karl glanced over at his alien slave girl, who merely shook her head as though urging him not to fight them.

Karl tossed his sword aside. He lifted his hands in the air. "I surrender."

"Good." Claymore pulled a stunner pistol and fired a blue pulse at Karl.

It had been a month since Denise had been captured and the processing of the prisoners was done. Soon she would be sold into servitude and all her memories would be sealed. Denise and the others were lined up in a row. Helena was quickly sold off to two men dressed in white robes, and several other girls went to different men as the sale went on.

Eventually, a man wearing a faded Koal jacket entered the room. He was a young man in his twenties with blue eyes and metallic copper hair. On his right hip, he had a revolver with an ivory handle, and on his left, he had a Japanese katana.

"Is there something in particular that you're looking for?" asked a man in a white suit.

He glanced over all the girls. "I'm looking for something small," he answered.

Denise now had a really bad feeling about this man. He turned and pointed at her.

"She's small enough."

"What do you mean 'small enough'?!" she yelled.

The man in white pulled out a slave control rod and pressed a blue gem on the device. Her silver bracelet turned blue and she felt a painful electrical charge run through her body.

She screamed and dropped to the floor.

"We'll have her stripped and we'll seal her memories right away," said the man in white.

"I'll take her as is," said the man in the Koal jacket.

"Are you sure about this?" asked the man in white. "It'll only take a minute, and she is a feisty one."

"I like them feisty," he answered.

Lord, help me! she prayed when she heard those words.

The man paid a hundred fifty thousand Titan Cronos for her.

He took her up a long elevator to a hanger, where she saw a crimson red ship.

His ship was shaped like a long thin triangle with a diamond shaped bow. On each side of its hull were flat crest shaped objects.

They boarded the crimson ship and ascended a spiral staircase to what she believed was the bridge.

The bridge was shaped like a long thin diamond with five chairs arranged at different points. The captain's chair was in the center of the bridge and slightly elevated above the others. Two seats were placed one on each side of the captain's seat. Directly in front of the captain's space was a reclining chair that was in a small pit area. The last seat was just behind the captain's chair.

There were three people on the bridge.

"Welcome aboard the *Crimson Blade*," said her new master. "This is Ray, our mechanic."

He pointed to an Asian boy who looked like he was about thirteen. "That's B-10, our helmsman."

He referred to a girl of about eighteen with long black hair and silver eyes. "That's Kira, our muscle."

Denise looked at the last person on the ship who was a little girl of about twelve years with white cat ears and a long white feline tail.

Ray stood up and walked over to the copper haired man with an agitated expression.

"Surge! What were you thinking?" asked the boy. "We don't need another crew member. What can she even do on this ship? B-10 can literally pilot this ship with her eyes closed. Kira could take out three Martian army squads without a weapon. I've worked on this ship so long that if I got a hold of the right materials I could rebuild the whole ship from scratch. Then you're a halfway decent swordsman and gunslinger. So other than for your sick enjoyment, there is no use for her."

"She is going to be our new cook," Surge answered, with a smile on his face.

"I'm what?!" she yelled.

"All right, you win," Ray said reluctantly, reminded of the fact that none of the other crew members could cook any food without making it poisonous to humans.

Surge smiled and settled back in his chair on the bridge. "Prepare to take off, B-10," he commanded.

"Hey, hold on a second!" yelled Denise.

"Set course for the Aris Asteroid Belt," he said, completely ignoring Denise.

B-10 relaxed in the recliner and the chair sank into the pit. "Connection established, ready for takeoff," she said, as her eyes started glowing white.

Ray and Kira jumped in their seats, leaving only the seat in the back. Denise started towards the chair. Suddenly there was a jolt and Denise was knocked to the floor.

"Didn't I tell you to sit down?" Surge stated, turning back to gape at her.

"No, you didn't," she responded, glaring at him as she climbed into the chair.

The walls of the bridge slid back revealing the hanger they were in. The roof of the hanger opened, letting in the icy wind of the planet. With another jolt, the ship lifted herself off the hanger floor and left the building. As they flew through the atmosphere, Denise saw how dark and frozen the surface of the planet was.

The ship flew into space.

"Ray, prepare to open a Dark Space corridor," said Surge, just before stars in front of the *Crimson Blade* vanished and the ship was absorbed into a starless void.

68

After a few moments, Denise could make out the dark red veins all around the vessel that outlined the tunnel. Suddenly, the ship struck one of the veins and everything in front of the ship turned red. Then the red was stripped away and replaced by pitch black. Stars started to appear again, revealing that they had returned to normal space.

"The ship has safely exited Dark Space," said B-10 as her irises returned to silver.

"How long before we can enter the next Dark Space Corridor?" asked Surge.

"Twelve hours before we reach the corridor to Aris," answered Ray.

"Autopilot is set," stated B-10. Her chair raised itself.

"Well, looks like we'll have to wait." Surge got out of his chair. He turned his head towards Denise and smiled. "Kira, could you take the new crew member to her quarters."

Kira jumped out of her seat and saluted. "Yes, sir." She grabbed Denise by the wrist and dragged her out of the chair.

Denise tried to pull herself free but the little brown-haired white-eared girl's grip was too powerful. They went down the staircase and into a black octagon shaped corridor.

The two of them stopped at a red door, which slid open, revealing a cabin with dangling ropes hanging all over the place and a bed that was only two feet below the ceiling. On the walls were the images of moving fish swimming in water.

"This is where you're going to be staying," Kira said with a cheerful tone. "This is technically my cabin, but you can have it. I sleep wherever I want anyways. And since we're the same size, you can borrow my clothes."

Denise crossed her arms, as her eye twitched slightly. Being reminded of her small size was one of the things that could really make Denise snap. However, since Kira was a little girl, she forced herself to let it slide.

"Bye. I have training to do." Kira left the room.

Denise was left alone in the room. This was going to be her room. The size was all right, but the main problem was that the bed was seven feet in the air. There was no way she would be able to get up there.

"Great." She saw a chair by the back wall, claimed it, and decided to rest her eyes.

Exhausted from everything, she quickly dozed off.

When Denise awoke, she was happy that she was not marrying that little boy in her nightmare. She stretched her arms, then got out of the chair and went down the dimly lit corridor.

Denise climbed the spiral staircase to the bridge.

There she found, to her surprise, that B-10 was still sitting in her chair with the lights off. Denise saw several glowing wires running under B-10's clothes and skin.

She turned and went back down the staircase.

As she advanced down the corridor, she tripped and fell over something large and cumbersome. Denise turned to see what she had tripped over.

Curled up on the floor was Kira.

She was undisturbed by Denise's fall and continued to sleep in the corridor making a noise that sounded like the cross between a purr and a snore.

Denise got up, deciding that it might be best to go back to the room that had been given to her.

On her way back, she noticed a light on in a room not far from hers.

She peered inside, where she found Surge raiding the ship's kitchen.

He looked up at her, his hand still on the refrigerator door.

"Hey, what are you lurking around here for?" he asked. "If you're hungry, you can help yourself."

"No, thanks. I'm fine," she said as her stomach growled. Once again, her body was demanding food against her will.

Eating is so exhausting.

"I can leave if you like," he informed her.

"You don't have to do that," she said, in an irritated tone of voice. "It's just that I don't like eating."

He stood there, dumbfounded.

"But my stupid body is demanding food."

He waited a few seconds before replying. "Well, what would it like?"

Surge had a surprisingly kind smile on his face.

70

Denise ended up cooking hamburgers for both Surge and herself.

"So, what is your full name?" Denise loaded her hamburger with ketchup. "Is Surge a first name, last name, or just something you thought was cool?"

"Surge is it," he answered. "It's my first name, last name, and title."

"Why do you have only one name?" she asked, being made curious by his statement.

"It just happened to be what I was calling myself when my old man took me in thirteen years ago. He never made me change it, so it just stuck. However, I may have a real name, but I have no idea what that is." He paused to take jelly out of the fridge.

"Why is that?" she asked.

"The thing is, I'm one of the people whose control bracelet was removed before the sentence was up," he said, pulling out what appeared to be cookie dough. "So I can't remember anything from before I was twelve. Fortunately, my old man was kind enough to take in a halfbreed before I got into real trouble."

The human girl had just gone from thinking that the bounty hunter was an obnoxious jerk to actually feeling sorry for him.

But his statement that he was a "halfbreed" was something that she did not totally understand.

"What exactly did you mean by the term halfbreed?" she asked, hoping he wouldn't take offense to the question.

"Can't you tell by my metallic copper hair and Terran eyes?" he stated like it was something really obvious. "Did you grow up in some metal tank out in deep space where you didn't learn how to tell the different races apart?"

"Actually, I did," she answered. "The world I came from was completely isolated and we really didn't learn about the happenings of the rest of the galaxy. And what the people in power did, I don't know, they didn't tell the general public. I learned more about the different races on the prison planet than anywhere else."

"Well," he stated, as he pulled out something that looked like mashed potatoes.

"So, now that we know a little bit about each other, what's the deal with the catgirl, the little boy, and the woman that has the silver eyes?"

"B-10 is a gynoid navigation unit from a retired Terran battleship that my stepbrother revived two years ago," he answered as he pulled out the chocolate syrup. "The catgirl is a member of a genetically engineered race of warriors known as the Lrakians. She fled her pride a year and a half ago and my old man recruited her just before he died. She hasn't ever told me about her past before then."

He pulled out something that looked like salsa.

"And the boy is my stepbrother, my old man's biological son who decided to join us shortly after the death of his mother."

He pulled out some fried rice and mixed it with the syrup.

"By the way, why do you need a cook anyway?" she asked.

Then she looked down at the things he was putting on his hamburger- grape jelly, mashed potatoes, chocolate syrup, salsa, cookie dough, and fried rice. She felt like she was going to throw up.

"I think I just answered my own question," she said, covering her mouth with her hand.

Now I remember why food is the enemy.

He took a bite out of his hamburger.

"This coming from someone who uses that nasty stuff called ketchup," he said, before taking another bite out of his food. "What? It all ends up in the same place."

"You're worse than my brother," she said, pushing her food away after only taking three bites. "I'm done."

She stormed out of the room.

"I'll never understand women," he commented just before he inhaled his food.

"Surge, you're needed on the bridge." B-10's voice came from a communication device on his belt. "We are ready to enter dark space."

"I'll be there in a minute," he replied.

He placed Denise's hamburger in a container and put it in the fridge before returning to the bridge.

Staring out a large window overlooking a fleet of long black triangular ships were the purple eyes of a man in a white coat.

His metallic gold hair was slicked back.

Gloves covered his hands, which were placed behind his back.

He was Jarl Narkren, Grand Protector of the Neith Federation.

Twelve years ago his government had succeeded the Neith

Empire, which had been ruled for well over a thousand years by the Sargoth Dynasty.

Overthrowing the weak inbred royal family had progressed quickly, thanks to the support of one of the Jovian states.

The new government was completely stable to the point that there seemed to be almost no one who would oppose the state, but new information had come to his attention that could derail everything.

A young man with copper hair entered the room.

Narkren turned to view him again. "Falgrom, how goes the search?" he asked.

"We located a girl matching her records."

"Have our operative in the area bring her to us, so we can see if she is indeed the real thing," he commanded.

He turned away and stared off into space again.

The young man just stood there quietly.

Narkren turned his head barked to the young man. "Is there a problem?"

The young man stood quietly for a second as though he was afraid to speak.

"Well," he said gulping. "We lost contact with our operative in the area."

"What!" Narkren yelled, punching the window with his fist.

Falgrom stepped back. "Well, some Terran bought her, and he said he was going to retrieve her once the Terran arrived."

Narkren gritted his teeth. "Send someone to retrieve her and take care of the Earthling," he said, turning back to the fleet. "If she is indeed Vlora, as the last heir to the Neith throne, then the entire nation could be ripped apart by civil war."

Karl awoke with a mass of yellow-orange fur covering half his face.

"Lightening, what are you doing on my face?" Karl pushed the cat off of him.

"It was very comfortable," Lightening answered. "Human bodies make great pillows when you aren't moving."

They were resting in a king sized canopy bed. Karl glanced to the right and saw his .45 automatic on a nightstand. Leaning against the doorway was his khopesh and sitting on a table was his bag containing his belongings from the Academy.

"All right, Lightening, what happened?" Karl asked the cat.

"Well, you got knocked out again." Lightening licked his belly.

Do I seriously have to be kidnapped and knocked out by everyone we encounter? Karl thought as he climbed out of bed. "Well, how did my stuff get here?"

"You might want to check and see if it's all there," said a woman's voice.

He turned to see Sophia in a bed on the left side of the room. Karl's entire body suddenly became hot all over. She stretched her arms. The only garments she wore were one of Karl's t-shirts from his school uniforms and a pair of short shorts.

"I'm sorry I went ahead and borrowed this shirt since I don't have any night clothes. By the way, why is your skin a lot pinker than usual?"

"Karl is one of those humans that turns pink when they get embarrassed." Lightening cleaned the place under his tail.

"Why would he be embarrassed?" she asked, somehow lacking an understanding of humans and their emotions.

"Because Karl comes from a culture where a girl sleeping in the same room with a guy, and then wearing his shirt, are considered to be things associated with a Meow relationship."

Her face suddenly turned bright yellow. "Why didn't you tell me that?" she asked, with a disturbed glare in her eyes.

"You never asked," Lightening answered. "Besides even if you're an alien you should have some idea of what happens when males and females get together."

74

After Karl and Sophia's faces went back to normal, Karl confirmed that most of his belongings were still there. The only possession missing was the Koal jacket.

Right, I used that jacket to pay for the docking fee on the Devil's Fang.

"So, what happened?" Karl asked the girl, knowing that the cat was not going to give him a decent answer.

"Claymore shot you," she answered. "After you were knocked out we agreed to negotiate with Claymore's business partner for your belongings and this room."

While he was happy to have his property back, he didn't like the idea of having to deal with Claymore. "Well, Sophia, what are our options?" Karl asked.

"I don't remember telling you that you could call me that," she stated.

"Some might take that as a sign of rebellion," he reminded her. "So, from now on your name is, Sophia Rubyeyes."

She smiled as she held up her control rod.

"You can't do anything without this," she replied, picking up the pistol. "And you can't take it from me if I have a gun. Now then, how much would you be willing to sell me for?"

"When did I say I was actually planning on selling you?" he asked, realizing the girl still had the safety on his .45 automatic.

"Just tell me," she said with agitation. "I want to know how much a one-armed Lecaran slave girl is worth to you."

"60, 000 credits," said Karl.

"What?!" asked the girl, surprised. "That's six times the appraised value. You can't expect to get that."

"Well, first there's the cost of buying you, then there's the cost of your clothes," he answered. "And the meal came to about 950 credits, also if you want to keep that gun, that's another thousand."

"That's 46,000 and most of that you spent on yourself," she stated. "Where does that get me to being worth 60,000?"

"Well, I'm counting the rest of it as paying for all the trouble I went through after buying you," he answered, leaning back in his chair.

"You greedy son of a-" Sophia immediately paused. "There's no need for you to throw my clothes and everything else into the price."

"I would be concerned." Lightening jumped on Karl's chest. "I didn't think Karl was the type who would suddenly have the need for women's clothing."

"And the cat just made my point," said Karl, scratching the cat's ear. "So you can either do 60,000 credits worth of work for me or come up with a way to make the money that doesn't involve anything from me."

She sighed. "All right then." She pulled out the silver garment Karl bought. "I'll get you the money you want, but the method may be somewhat on the unscrupulous side. I think I'll go relax. Let's go to the hotel's hot tub."

Karl waited several minutes in the large hot tub. As he started to wonder about how the others were doing, Sophia finally came out of the changing room. She was wearing a dark blue one piece bathing suit and slid into the water beside Karl, whose heart rate suddenly went up again.

"Do you really have a problem with me calling you Sophia?" he asked, trying to break the silence more than anything else.

"Not really," she answered, keeping her left arm raised to keep her damaged wrist out of the water. "Just remember, I'm not going to give you back the control rod."

"Keep it." Karl put his hands behind his head. "I don't know how that thing works anyway. So, have you found out anything about yourself from that rod?"

"Not much," she answered, grabbing her left elbow to support her mechanical arm. "But for some reason dancing and starship piloting are on my skill list along with basic housekeeping skills."

"Starship piloting might come in handy," Karl stated, looking up at the ceiling which had been given the appearance of a night sky.

Now if I could only get back to my ship. Suddenly Karl remembered the *Devil's Fang,* which he had left on Dainare III. He figured he should probably check on her. "So what exactly are the rules for relations between men and women who are not related where you come from?" he asked, trying to avoid any more awkward situations with this girl.

"Well, in the former Empire of Neith, marriages of the lower classes were arranged between families of unrelated bloodlines on a regular basis," she answered, sliding deeper into the warm water.

"Too bad, Karl," said Lightening. He was curled up on a stack of towels sitting near the hot tub. "Arranged marriages only. Though, I suppose, as your guardian I could negotiate with you as the girl's master, I would have to approve your marriage to her and you would have to approve her marriage to you." Lightening paused for a moment to lick the base of his tail. "You humans have to make everything so complicated."

"The former nobility, however," Sophia disregarded the cat's statements and continued on, "of the empire consisted of the handful of families who consistently married off first and second cousins to each other. And that inbreeding is what led to the fall of the Sargoth Dynasty. The entire nobility was sold into slavery and their memories were sealed."

"Well," Karl said with a smile on his face. "I had no idea you were an aristocrat."

She giggled after that statement. "It's terrible," she stated while trying to keep a straight face. "That would explain why I know I'm from Neith."

"You could even be a lost princess," he said as a joke.

"I wouldn't joke about that. The Neith Federation put all the royal family members they could find to death. If one were still alive, they would become the most wanted Lecaran in the Galaxy," she said, trying to get him to keep his mouth shut about things that might result in her death. "That man from earlier may have only been looking for something to put in a house of ill repute, but he might have been after me because of something my family did in the past." She glanced down at her left arm. "A prosthetic like this isn't something a slave would be walking around with. So I must have been connected with someone that had money."

Karl moved in front of Sophia and examined her arm. "I can't even tell that arm apart from a real one," he said, grabbing her left hand. It even felt real, the only thing giving it away was the gash in the side of her wrist which exposed the metal framework and wiring in her hand

"I'll be happy when I regain the feeling of these two fingers," she stated, looking at the twitching of her pinky and ring fingers. "Since you are so curious about me I hope you don't mind telling me a little bit about the person who calls himself my master?"

"Well in 1912, I was partnered with a British secret agent on board the *Titanic*," Lightening said, licking his paw. "Then I was working with a con artist turned millionaire private detective, and I just skipped over the 1970s. After that I was with some people that crossed over into another dimension where a friend of mine got hold of a magic sword. I was also involved with a warrior from the last Zodiac War and I can't tell you anything else."

Both Karl and the girl were astonished to hear what came out of Lightening's mouth.

Karl smirked. What Lightening said just made what he was about to say a little less odd.

"Well, I was born in one of the colony ships that was launched into deep space after the invasion of Earth. My colony ship came under attack and I ended up here."

She became solemn for a moment.

"You aren't shocked by any of this?"

"Not really," she answered. "What the cat said is really out there, but what you said happened to you is indeed very possible. The thing I don't understand. If you're from one of the lost tribes of the Terran invasion, why don't you harbor any ill will against me?"

"I see no point in it. The ones who attacked Earth are long dead," he said, assuming that the Lecarans did not have a different life span than humans.

The girl just sat quietly, which started to worry Karl.

"They are dead, right? There isn't some immortal emperor who has been ruling for centuries, is there?"

She giggled. "No, Sargoth Vearas died at the age of 109 years," she said, still laughing at his comment. "Her descendants, on the other hand, with the exception of the Princess Vlora, were killed in the Neith Revolution years ago."

Claymore's two Lecaran friends entered the pool area, and with them was a metallic copper haired woman wearing black pants and a tank top.

"Never thought I'd see the day when a Lecaran and a Terran would get along so well," said the yellow eyed woman to the two men of her race.

"I saw it all the time back in the empire," stated the older man.

"Many of the Neith nobles became infatuated with their Terran slaves. However in this case, I do not think it is a good idea for us to let this continue, Ellris." The older man ran his finger across his eyebrow.

"I understand, master," the younger man answered.

"I'll never understand the two of you," said the young woman. "But I don't think we need to mess with their little romance."

"This has nothing to do with you, Zrela," said the older man.

"Calidi, you really are a purest, aren't you?" said Zrela. She left Ellris and Calidi, walking off towards the women's changing room.

The older Lecaran glared at Zrela as she left. "To have to serve on the same ship as someone like her," Calidi stated to his younger companion. "Running around dressed like a Terran woman. She doesn't know anything about being a proper lady."

Calidi's point was demonstrated when she came out wearing a small bright red bikini. Zrela darted from the changing room and made a cannon ball into the pool, showering Karl and Sophia with water.

Meanwhile, Lightening spied a button on a Karl's handheld and placed his paw on it. The holographic words appeared about above the object that read "room service".

"Room service, how may we help you?" asked a voice.

"Well, I'd like some ham sliced into tiny cubes, then covered in spaghetti sauce," Lightening ordered, licking his lips. "Oh, and bring a bowl of shrimp."

"And who do I charge it to?"

"Ashley Claymore. Account number 7372258," answered the cat.

Sitting in a large dimly lit room was a relatively young man in a white coat, with long metallic silver hair tied back in a ponytail. His ruby red eyes were fixed on the portrait of two little girls with metallic gold hair and eyes, the same as his.

"Who're they supposed to be?" asked a bald white Terran man who stood about seven feet tall and had an enormous sword strapped on his back. "I see what looks like an eight-year-old and a fourteen-year-old."

"They're princesses of the Neith Royal family," Baldassara answered. "The younger one is Vearas and the older one is Vlora." He turned his head and looked Thorn straight in the eye. "The painting by the famous artist, Deborah D Russo, was smuggled off Venus before it could be destroyed by the new regime. It's been many days since that portrait was painted. If they were alive, what beauties they would have become."

"But the fall of that dynasty was over a decade ago," Thorn commented.

The Lecaran paused for a moment.

"I forgot you measure time by how long it takes your original planet to revolve around the orb of light," Baldassara stated. "Not by the rotation of your world."

"I fail to see why your kind took that godforsaken planet as your capital after stealing Earth," Thorn said with a bitter tone. "The days are longer than the years."

"True, the surface pressure is still capable of crushing any humanoid," Baldassara replied. "But during the empire, Venus was quite beautiful from the sky citadels. What treasures were left behind when-"

"Treasure." The Terran licked his lips. "Guess, I'll have to wait till I get off this asteroid before I can have any fun."

Thorn left the room.

"I thought he would never leave," said a woman sitting in the shadows. Her eyes were hidden from view by the hood of a purple cloak. However, based on what was visible, she was a very beautiful Lecaran with long silver hair. "I detest his kind."

"Nara, I am afraid the Triad has rejected my plan to assault the Chapel of Ralethim." Baldassara rose from his chair. "Which means that there is something I am going to need for my plans to succeed."

"What is it, my lord?" she asked.

"I need you to help me locate the former grand princess of the Neith Empire, Vlora." He pulled a small one-handed axe with a crystal blade out of his desk.

"I thought all members of the Sargoth's family were killed with the Sargoth himself," she stated.

"That's what most people believe," said Baldassara, with a look of superiority on his face. "However, from the information I collected, it appears that Vlora was not even at the execution, and the Neith Federation has spent almost half a generation hunting for her. If it got out that Vlora was still alive, the old supporters of the royal family might start a rebellion to restore the old monarchy. So only a few people were allowed to know that Vlora was never at the execution." The handle of the glass axe extended and became a six feet long halberd. "This is a weapon given only to the bodyguards of the royal family. With this you should be about to earn the trust of those who served the old monarchy."

She knelt before him. "Under the Great Lord, I shall serve no other," said Nara, as she received the halberd from his hand. She stood up and retracted the halberd back into a one-handed axe. "What of Thorn? He is loyal to the Triad."

"The bounty hunter will take care of him," he stated, glancing over at a semitransparent image of a small crimson ship. "Ready the *Vearas*. It's time for us to leave."

The *Crimson Blade* entered the asteroid belt of the Aris System.

From the bridge, Denise saw a large gray ship with a claw shaped bow and two short cylinders on the sides of her long hexagon shaped hull.

"The *Vearas*," stated Surge.

"Shall we lay in pursuit?" B-10 asked.

"Don't bother, that ship's about to flash," Ray stated.

A minute or so later, a bluish-white flash streaked from the bow to the stern leaving behind nothing of the *Vearas*.

"What was that?" Denise asked.

"That was a ship belonging to the Syndicate pirate, Baldassara," Surge answered. "Ray, can you tell where she came from?"

Ray began to type on his console.

A screen with the image of an asteroid appeared in front of them. The asteroid had a small port built into the rock face, which a large ship like the *Vearas* would have barely fit in, but it had more than enough room for the *Crimson Blade*.

The *Crimson Blade* went into stealth mode and Ray hacked the port's systems allowing them to dock in the asteroid. Surge, Kira, and Ray left the ship and moved into a base built into the asteroid. B-10 was left in charge of the ship and watching Denise.

"So, what are we going to do?" Denise asked.

B-10 reached under her chair and pulled out a book and began reading.

Denise was left to boredom, with nothing to read, watch, play, or anyone to talk to.

She contemplated how bizarre life had become.

She was on a ship run by a half alien bounty hunter who was hunting pirates, and ate like someone without any taste buds.

But he was kind of cute.

Karl was once again dressed in a brown suit with his .45 under his vest. He picked up the glass khopesh he had taken earlier from the Lecaran, who tried to kill him, and attached it to his belt.

Lightening was sitting on the bed. He was thinking about his next meal and licking his lips.

Sophia came out of the bathroom in a sleeveless black dress with a gold chain acting as a belt.

Karl noticed that she was wearing black heels instead of her glass shoes.

Sophia picked up her purse and they went downstairs to a party that Zrela had told them about earlier.

They entered the party room, which Karl believed to be an underground casino for illegal betting.

"Karl, remember parties are nothing but trouble," Lightening said, reminding him of the October 31st attack on the Galaxy Academy aboard the *Nomad.*

"I remember, Lightening." Karl scratched the cat's head.

Most of the forms of gambling Karl recognized, like card games, slot machines, and roulette wheels.

There were also things that he had never seen before involving holographic puppets, floating swords, and energy balls, none of which made any sense to him.

Sophia walked over to a bar which had been set up as an exchange point for getting casino chips, something which had been out of use since the mid twenty-first century.

She pulled her glass shoes out of her purse and exchanged them for five rows of blue chips.

"What are you doing?" asked Karl.

"You said if I got you 60,000 I would be a free woman," she answered, before handing him half of her chips. "This brings it down to 55,000." Sophia went towards a table with a strange energy ball flashing different colored lights.

Karl and Lightening went off and looked around on their own.

In addition to not wanting to risk losing money, the only game Karl could play was blackjack. And he did not see a blackjack table.

After a couple of minutes of wandering aimlessly, he discovered Jacob and Justin, who unlike him, were back to wearing their Galaxy Academy uniforms.

Both of them were dueling in a game with holographic swords.

Jacob was armed with a claymore, and Justin was armed with two katanas.

Their opponent was a Koal and in the alien's hand was a holographic rapier.

Unlike the others, Karl saw this Koal's helmet was more form fitting and moved with the neck rather than being fused to the shoulders.

Running at the Koal, Jacob raised his sword above his head.

Before he even got a chance to swing, the holographic rapier went through his heart.

Jacob's claymore disappeared as the armored figure removed the sword from his chest.

Justin came at the alien, holding his swords together like a pair of scissors.

The Koal moved gracefully out of the way and stabbed him in the neck.

Jacob and Justin got up from their mock battle and walked away with disgusted looks on their faces.

Karl proceeded to the dueling floor.

"The betting starts at 500 credits," said a female voice coming from the Koal.

"There will be no spitting, hitting between the legs, or use of dishonorable tactics in the fight."

A woman? Karl thought. *I wonder what she looks like under that armor.*

The swords were holographic and could not inflict real harm on a person. However, the chip placed on the back of the neck simulated the pain of a sword strike until the end of the battle. The player first to eliminate their opponent's hit points was the winner.

A cylinder, with the diameter of a soda can, rose out of the floor beside him.

Karl removed his jacket and vest, then slid two casino chips into the cylinder. A flap on the side of the cylinder popped open, holding a small triangular chip.

Karl picked up the chip and placed it on the back of his neck.

"Name your sword of choice." He pulled out his sickle sword, of which he was already becoming fond.

"I'll go with this." He placed the sword beside his jacket.

"Load khopesh," said the girl with the rapier.

An almost perfect replica of his sword appeared in his hand.

If it were not for the ghostlike appearance of the weapon, he would not have been able to tell it was a hologram.

She held her sword in front of her face. "Reginia Craen," she stated. "It is customary to give your name before a duel, even in a fake one like this."

"Karl Sabers," he said, with a smile on his face.

They took a fencing stance.

Each waited for the other to move.

Karl had seen how easily she was able to beat the two unsophisticates from the *Nomad.*

He was not about to let the same thing happen to him.

Reginia moved forward with a thrust of her sword.

Karl deflected her attack with his khopesh.

She kicked the side of his right leg, knocking him off his feet.

He rolled to his left before her blade pierced him.

He jumped to his feet and backed away.

"Shall we raise the stakes?" asked Reginia.

He placed another chip in the slot, leaving only a 5,000 credit chip in his pocket.

Karl charged at her with his sword pointed. Just like with Jacob, she moved out to strike from the side.

Karl turned and prevented the sword from striking his neck.

Her blade was only inches away from him and pierced his left shoulder.

As her blade slid further into his shoulder, he quickly shifted his sword to his left and slashed her across the chest.

Her rapier vanished and the pain in his arm did the same. Six casino chips popped out of the cylinder on Karl's side.

Karl pulled the chip on the back of his neck off and picked up his belongings.

"So, what are you going to do next?" asked Lightening. "Gamble away all your money like an idiot or do the smart thing and get me something to eat."

"I think I'm done gambling," Karl answered, smiling at the ten chips he had won. He glanced back at the Koal woman, who he suspected looked quite displeased under her mask. "I better quit while I'm ahead. Let's see if we can find Sophia."

Karl and Lightening found Sophia playing poker with Ashley, Ellris, and Calidi.

Sitting beside her was a large stack of casino chips.

The other players were not doing too well. Most of their chips were gone.

She stood up, put her chips in a tray, and walked away.

Karl started towards her.

"Hey, Terran," said Calidi, as he stepped in front of Karl. "Are you that girl's owner?"

"Depends," Karl answered. "What's it to you?"

"I'd like to buy her," stated the Lecaran man. "I'll give you 50,000 Titan Cronos for her."

Karl went around Calidi and walked away without saying anything.

"Fine then, 60,000."

Karl turned his head.

"I don't think it's going be possible now," he stated. "I've already promised her to someone else, so you'll have to talk to her about it."

"Just who are you selling her to?" he asked, with an aggravated tone in his voice. "What kind of person would pay that much for a girl like her?"

"You'll have to ask her," Karl said, pointing at Sophia, who came back with her glass shoes and one of those computers that looked like a hockey puck. "Got the money?"

"You're selling her to herself?" asked Calidi, perturbed.

Karl looked at his handheld and saw that the rest of the money had already been transferred.

"Well, looks like she's already changed hands," Karl said, to Calidi. "So, why did you want to buy her anyway?"

Calidi left in disgust after hearing that turn of events and returned to his companions.

Karl exchanged the chips for Titan Cronos.

As he picked up his money from the humanoid robot at the counter, he felt something cold touch the side of his neck.

"Have you forgotten the business meeting you were supposed to attend?" said a tan skinned young woman with dark brown hair.

She had a pistol pointed at Karl's neck.

She reached into Karl's vest and took his .45.

Sophia and Lightening went towards the door but were stopped by Calidi and Ellris.

The captives were then brought to a table where they were introduced to another Lecaran friend of Claymore's.

This friend's eyes were bright red and his hair, once gold, had turned almost entirely black with age.

"So what do you want with us?" asked Karl.

"If it has nothing to do with food, we're not interested," Lightening said, rubbing against Karl's legs.

"I am Captain Gavorlo Micalo.". "I want the two of you to join my crew onboard the *Lady Eris*. From what I heard from my business partner, Ashley, you're currently serving onboard the *Starlight*, which makes you very useful for my work." He put his hands together and smiled.

"So?" asked Karl with a suspicious tone in his voice. "What kind of ship would take an ex-slave and a ship jumper?"

"A pirate ship," Sophia stated. "You're after access codes for Karl's ship."

"Correct," answered Micalo. "Smart girl, too bad you're not as valuable as him."

"Since I am of no value," she stated, before turning to leave. "I will respectfully decline your offer."

Micalo pulled out a black curved pistol and pointed it a Sophia.

"You'll be coming with us, young lady," said the pirate, looking quite pleased with himself. "Now, if you don't want to join us, then I could always make arrangements for you to meet with my good friend Ashley Claymore. He was quite interested you, and now that you no longer have a master…"

Chapter 11- The Raid

Two men, dressed in black armor with helmets adorned with a single red lens over the left eye, stood guard. They were armed with K-12s, a weapon that was both a 1,000-round assault rifle and a semiautomatic mini rocket launcher. As a sidearm, they had rods that would coat themselves in plasma, making them able to cut through nearly anything. They were standing guard in front of the double doors leading into Baldassara's office.

One of the guards detected something moving quickly across his scanners. "What was that?" asked the guard.

"Me," answered Kira, stretching herself in front of them. "Meow."

Recognizing her as a Lrakian, they immediately opened fire on her. Kira leaped into the air and landed on the face of the one of the guards, then kicked the other in the neck.

"Wow," said Ray, smiling at Kira while scratching the back of his head. "You went easy on them."

"All right, all right," said Surge. "Let's stop wasting time and get back to work." They headed into Baldassara's office.

Ray investigated a set of controls built into Baldassara's chair.

"Ray, can you access their main systems from here?"

"Yeah, but it might take some time," he answered, looking at the controls.

"Well, hurry," said the bounty hunter. "It looks like they don't know we're here, but that could change any minute."

Ray was able to hack in far quicker than he predicted. As it turned out, the reason it had been so easy getting this far wasn't because they weren't detected by the pirates, but because the base was almost completely empty. The pirates were no longer interested in the base and were abandoning it. The only pirate that even had a high bounty on his head was the one called, Thorn.

"Damn it!" Surge said, punching the wall. "We lost him."

"Well," began Ray, stretching his arms. "If we can at least get Thorn, this trip will be worth it."

"Guess I'll have to settle for him." Surge said, gritting his teeth. "Where is he?"

Ray gasped at the location on the screen. "He's headed for the

Crimson Blade!"

"WHAT?!" yelled Surge. "I thought we had her cloaked!" He pulled out his handheld. "B-10, move the ship and raise the shields." Unfortunately, Surge's command was intercepted by a hacker working for the pirates, and rewritten before it got to the *Crimson Blade.*

"B-10, the job's taken care of, come on out," it read at delivery.

B-10 heard the message and noticed there were slight discrepancies in Surge's voice. After calculating a five percent chance that the video was forged, she tried raising the ship's shields, but her efforts were in vain. The shield generator was not responding and the engines were also dead.

She detected something moving in the lower deck and grabbed two pistol-sized machine guns.

"What are you doing?" asked Denise. She got out of her chair. "Are you planning on going out?"

"The pirates know we are here," answered B-10. "And I believe they are boarding."

"Then give me a gun," said Denise.

"Negative," replied B-10. "Organics should never fire range weapons onboard ships."

Denise followed B-10 as they went through the long dark hexagon shaped corridor of the vessel.

The situation was starting to freak out Denise. It had the same feel as a horror movie. At any moment, a monster or a psychopath could leap out from the next corner and kill them. A few seconds later the blade of a huge sword went through B-10's abdomen. Connected to the sword was Thorn, who stood there grinning at his work. Denise screamed as he pulled his sword out of B-10, then quickly grabbed Denise by the neck and dragged her through the open hatch on the bottom of the *Crimson Blade.* Denise struggled and screamed for help as he brought her into the hanger where he was joined by at least twenty of his pirate comrades.

Once outside, Thorn dropped her on the floor and placed his hands on her torso. She continued to struggle and prayed that something would stop this from happening.

How could these people just sit there while this is happening?!
Do they get some sort of sick enjoyment out of this?!

The sound of rapid gunfire rang out, and Denise saw all of

Thorn's fellow pirates drop to the floor, each of them with a single bullet hole in the forehead. Denise and Thorn looked up to see B-10 standing outside the *Crimson Blade* with a one foot long vertical wound on the left side of her abdomen.

"Target is using personal shield to deflect bullet," said B-10 with an emotionless tone in her voice. "Target identified as Derekson Thorn, an E-Class cyborg wanted on counts of piracy, murder, and inflicting damage on the gynoid unit designated as B-10."

"Hey?!" Thorn reacted to the fact that B-10 was counting the harm he just inflicted on her among his crimes. "Damaging robots is not a crime in most systems."

"Target is wanted dead or alive," she stated with a cold tone in her voice. "Destroy mode activated."

She dropped her guns, then rushed at Thorn with inhuman speed and kicked him in the chest. As he was thrown back several feet, he lost his huge sword. He tried to get up but was knocked back to the ground by B-10's fist. While he was on the ground, she decided to kill him with one kick to the neck.

However, Thorn was back on his feet faster than B-10 calculated. He grabbed her leg as she tried to kick him, then swung her in the air and slammed her into the hard metal floor.

Thinking she was dead, he left B-10 in the large dent that was made when he slammed her to the ground. He then saw Denise running towards an open corridor. With the power of his mechanical legs, he jumped into the air and landed directly in front of her, causing her to shriek. He smiled, before picking her up by her shirt.

As he brought her closer to him, a gold blast hit the energy shield around his body. Thorn and his hostage turned to see Surge standing before them with the open mouth of his katana's dragon head pointed at Thorn.

"Let the girl go!" Surge demanded, with a hate-filled tone in his voice.

"No!" Thorn shouted, looking at Denise. "This adorable little girl is insurance." He then held Denise in front of him like a shield.

"Adorable little girl?!" Denise yelled, fear leaving her. Anger and rage took its place. After everything that had happened with the *Nomad's* attack, being sold into slavery, having to see how that captain jerk ate, then to have this overgrown psycho try to violate her, calling her a "little girl" sent her off the edge. Not caring anything about the consequences of her actions, she kicked Thorn between the legs as hard as she could, with her own little battle cry.

Thorn loosened his grip on Denise's shirt as he dropped to his knees in pain. Denise was only free for a second before Thorn grabbed her leg and threw her about ten feet into the air. She closed her eyes, not screaming, and braced herself for the painful crash into the metal floor, however, she felt nothing. She opened her eyes and found herself in the arms of B-10.

She almost felt disappointed that she wasn't in the arms of Surge, but she quickly ran any thoughts like that out of her head.

As B-10 landed on the floor with Denise in her arms, Surge and Thorn stared at each other for several minutes. A long wire shot out of Thorn's right hand and wrapped around the hilt of his huge sword, then pulled the sword back to his hand. He rushed at Surge, swinging his sword. Surge moved out of the way of the massive sword and then pulled his katana from its scabbard.

Surge activated his sword's charge-cutter, turning the blade dark blue before he sliced off Thorn's mechanical right hand. Thorn raised his left fist to strike Surge, but before he had a chance, Surge split Thorn's arm from his knuckles to his elbow and took out both his legs in the same strike.

With his cybernetic limbs severed, Thorn fell flat on his back. Surge held his sword to Thorn's neck. "Where is Baldassara?"

"I don't know where he is," Thorn answered. "We were supposed to receive the location of the new base after it was established."

"Then I guess I have no more use for you." Surge sighed. The blade of his katana turned light blue and he cut the side of Thorn's neck. Thorn closed his eyes and became motionless. "B-10, take him back to the ship."

"Did you kill him?" asked Denise, as B-10 dragged Thorn away.

"No," he answered. "He's just stunned."

"You should have killed him," she stated, crossing her arms.

Surge turned off the charge-cutter field covering his sword and his sword instantly broke into several pieces.

Surge stood looking at his katana with his eyes wide open in shock.

"Just to let you know," Ray said, with some kind of handheld device in his hand, seemingly calculating something. "That is coming out of your share of the bounty."

Karl would have liked to have had time to decide whether he was going to accept the offer from Micalo.

But with pirates, saying "no" was frequently not an option.

Both Karl and Sophia were forced to join the crew of *The Lady Eris*, Micalo's pirate ship.

The two of them were taken to a large cargohold onboard *The Lady Eris*. It looked as though Micalo had assembled the entire crew. Many of these people Karl had met in the casino. The Koal woman, Reginia Craen, Calidi, Ellris, and Zrela were all members of Micalo's crew. Also there was a rock group called the Clearances.

Among the aliens were three Terran men, who Karl had not seen before.

There was a young man with a red monocle.

Beside him was a black man dressed in a gray suit.

Also, a blonde haired man stood at the right hand of the pirate captain.

Micalo stood in the center of the cargohold with Karl and Sophia.

"Today I would like to welcome two new additions to our crew," he said, to the ragtag group, as he pointed at Karl. "This is Karl Sabers, who has proven himself a fair swordsman and man lacking prejudice towards those of other races." He looked at Sophia. "And this is Sophia-" He paused a moment before he leaned over to the girl. "Hey, girl, what's your surname?" the captain asked in a whisper.

"I don't have one," she stated with a perturbed tone in her voice.

Micalo sighed. "Sophia Unknown, who has shown herself to be a capable gambler. And if nothing else, she makes the crew look all the prettier." He received a chuckle from his crew. He turned to the blonde man at his side. "Mr. Long, bring forth the codes."

"Aye, Captain," Long said, heading to the back of the crew.

A few minutes later Mr. Long returned with a ragged sheet of paper. Inscribed on the paper was-

The Codes of **The Lady Eris**
We the crew of **The Lady Eris** *establish these codes to prevent any strife among ourselves. Every entity that signs these codes is*

bound by them under the risk of the gray punishment.

Code 1- A crew member shall view members of the crew as family and shall never seek to betray fellow crew members.

Code 2- A crew member shall never murder a fellow crew member and any duel shall not be held on the ship.

Code 3- A crew member shall never steal from another crew member or take from the loot before receiving his share.

Code 4- A crew member shall never lust after another crew member's romantic partner.

Code 5- The loot should first be devoted to the upkeep of the ship, second to aid the wounded, and the rest shall be divided evenly among crew.

Code 6- The captain will be chosen by the crew.

Both Karl and Sophia signed the codes. Then the assembled crew let out cheers and shouts of joy.

In accordance with the code, Sophia was brought to Gavin, the mechanic, to have the damage she received to her left arm repaired, Lightening and Karl followed her because lunch wasn't available.

They entered a workshop filled with various types of machines ranging from dismantled post twenty-first century firearms to half constructed humanoid robots.

Gavin examined her arm and found that the damage to her left wrist had become worse with the cut in her synthetic skin, tearing open a hole now exposing the metal fibers running through the artificial muscle tissue and the black metal bones of her arm.

"I'm going to have to remove it," said Gavin as lights and symbols flashed across his monocle. "The arm should be fixed in about half a day."

Sophia wasn't too happy about letting some Terran pirate remove her arm, but using it in its current state was more of a handicap than just having one arm.

Gavin gripped the small area between the silver rings on her left arm with his index finger and thumb, then twisted it until it made a click. The arm detached, leaving the top silver ring, holding a metal plate at the end of her stub.

Sophia put on a jacket.

She and Karl proceeded out the door to where the dark skinned man wearing a gray suit stood outside waiting for them.

"I'm Henry Hunter," he introduced himself. "I'll be escorting you to your cabin."

They followed him down the corridor to a cabin which was slightly bigger than the ones on the *Starlight* and had only two bunks.

"Well, it's not much, but this is where you will be staying for now."

"So where's my room?" asked Karl.

"This is it," he stated. "The two of you are sharing a cabin. Have fun." Henry walked away with a smile on his face.

Karl did not exactly feel comfortable with the idea of sharing the same room with a girl.

It was not like he found her unattractive, but generally this situation was linked with an activity which he found morally wrong.

Sophia sat down on the left bunk.

"Aren't you bothered by this?" asked Karl.

"Of course, I am," she answered, removing her shoes and pulling the covers over her. "It's very annoying not having two arms."

"I still don't know how you humans connect sharing the same space with Meow," Lightening stated, as he entered the room and the door closed behind him.

Sophia popped up, with her face bright yellow. "Is it proper for Terran men and women to even be around each other?"

"Yes," Karl answered. "They just don't share the same bathrooms, living space, or beds, unless they are people engaged in physical relations."

"Within the Neith empire those who engaged in physical relations, become man and wife from that point on," she stated. "But sharing the same room, or using the same bed, are not considered a problem."

"Well, I guess that works," said Karl. He stretched out on his bunk. "In Ancient Texas they used to have it to where a man and a woman could be considered married just by living together."

He waited a few seconds for a response, but none came.

He glanced in her direction and saw that she had already passed out.

Lightening hopped on the bed, plopped down on Karl's arm, and went to sleep.

Chapter 12- Date with an Alien

Wrapped in a towel, Denise stepped out of the small bathroom into her cabin, She had felt the urge to take a shower after her encounter with that pervert, Thorn. She walked over to the chair she had left her clothes on, but they were gone. She heard the sliding of the cabin door and dashed into the bathroom. To her relief, Kira was the only one who came through the doorway.

"Kira, where are my clothes?" Denise asked, poking her head out of the bathroom.

"They needed to be washed," answered the catgirl. Kira opened a dresser drawer and pulled out a dark blue sleeveless dress. "You can wear this." Kira held the dress up in front of Denise and smiled.

"Thank you, but I'd be okay with a pair of pants and a shirt." Denise hadn't actually worn a dress in several years and didn't want to start now. "And what do you mean the clothes I had just put out needed to be washed?"

"You'll look cuter in the dress," Kira stated with an innocent air, ignoring the question about the missing clothes.

"No, thanks," Denise said, receding into the bathroom. Kira ran into the bathroom before the door had a chance to close. "Kira? What are yo..? Stop, Kira! NO, KIRA...!!!"

The Crimson Blade pulled into the docking bay of the saucer-shaped space station orbiting the yellow planet, Gleratice V.

Getting the bounty for Thorn was a simple matter. Hand him over to the Titan Military Police, and return with the money.

Surge went down to the lower deck where Ray was waiting with the three foot by five foot metal box that contained Thorn.

"Is that all of him?" Surge asked, looking at Ray with a suspicious glare. "You kept parts of him didn't you?"

"His head and torso are in there," Ray stated. "I can make good use of his arms and legs."

"Well, then, I'll be on my way," Surge said, as he placed his hand on the box. The box lifted off the ground and followed Surge as he walked towards the boarding ramp.

"I can't just let you take off by yourself," said Ray, with a serious tone in his voice.

"I thought you had to stay and fix B-10," answered Surge, looking back at him. "And find out how the pirates hacked our system?"

"That's right. And since Kira needs her catnap," he said, with a devious smirk on his face, "Denise will have to babysit you."

"What?" Surge asked, as Kira pushed Denise into the cargohold. Denise was wearing the blue dress that belonged to Kira. In an instant Surge, Denise, and their prisoner were forced out of the ship.

"You kids have fun!" Kira said, waving at them, as the bottom hatch raised itself into place.

"And don't spend any money!" said Ray, before the hatch completely closed.

The two walked through the checkpoint where they delivered Thorn to the Terran officers at the station. After picking up their reward money, Surge and Denise made their way into the city within the station. While the ceiling covering the city was not even high enough for buildings over ten stories, the image of the night sky had been projected over it to relieve any claustrophobic feelings the people within might experience. To Denise's surprise, the city itself was lit up with colors and many of the buildings varied in hues.

As they strolled down the street, Surge spotted a café. "So, do you want to get something to eat?"

"No!" she answered, remembering what he did with the hamburger she made. "I'm not hungry right now. Let's go somewhere else." She grabbed his arm and tried to drag him away. Then a loud rumble came from her stomach. *You had to do that now?! I'm not in the mood to eat!* she thought, glaring at her belly.

"You're not hungry, huh?" he asked, with a smile on his face.

"My body is forcing me to eat against my will," she stated. "If we find something else to do, it'll pass."

"We can't have that." He maneuvered her towards the café.

"No, I don't want to go!" Denise protested in vain as she was dragged into the restaurant. Surge flung out a chair and forced her to sit down.

"Go ahead and order." Surge sat down and looked at one of the holographic menus that appeared before them.

Denise sighed as she glanced at the menu in front of her. Upon seeing the language on the menu, she was confused and didn't understand. But after about half a minute, she could read the strange language. While her new language skill did disturb her some, she tried to push it out of her mind. She figured it was something which the people on Darkfour did to her, so there was nothing she could do about it. She ordered a personal pizza and Surge ordered a bowl of chili, bowl of chocolate ice cream, and a plate of catfish. Denise tried not to think about what he was going to do with his food. At best she figured his bad eating habits were from his alien background, but she wasn't totally sure about that.

"Hey, Surge?" she asked, as they waited for their food. He looked up at her. "Can you tell me something about your people?"

"The Terran or Lecaran." He sounded annoyed.

"Uh- the Lecarans?"

"All right, but I don't know a lot, nor do I have an interest in finding out," he stated. "As best I know, the Lecarans originated on a world called Lecara, and when the planet became too dangerous for them, they left and formed star kingdoms, based on the nations of their world. Then you have the unfriendly history that engulfed the relations between the Terrans and the Lecarans."

"So, is there any truth to the statement about the Lecarans being an imitation of the Terrans?" she asked curiously, thinking back to what the woman on Darkfour told her.

He sighed. "Did someone in a red uniform tell you that?" Surge asked.

Denise nodded meekly.

"You can't believe anything Blood Terra says. I won't exactly say how the Lecarans came to be. Some Terrans hold the preinvasion belief that all real life forms naturally evolved, and quite a few Lecarans believe that they were made them from the soil of Lecara. As for who's right, I really don't care. By the standards of both races I'm a flawed existence."

His statement just made her feel sorry for him, and she couldn't think of anything to say. Then the humanoid robot carrying a tray with their food arrived at the table. Denise ate a slice of her pizza before Surge mixed all his food in one bowl. Surge raised his hand in the air. "Hey, can I get some bacon and mayonnaise?" he asked the robotic waiter.

Denise dropped her second slice of pizza back on her plate when she heard Surge's request. "I've lost my appetite."

After Surge had consumed his mixture of different foods, he and Denise left the restaurant. Denise carried the three slices she couldn't finish in an insulated box, with plans to eat them later.

With his stomach filled, Surge decided it would be a good idea to start looking for a new katana. They stopped at the first weapon shop they came across. They stepped through the open doorway into a store with shelves stocked with pistols, rifles, and swords of nearly every type. Surge walked over to a large rack lined with katanas. He grabbed one of the swords in its scabbard with his left hand. Holding the weapon at his side with the scabbard's curve angled towards him, he gripped the hilt with his right hand. With lightning speed, he drew the sword and looked at the blade. He put that katana back and picked up another, repeating the action until he found a sword he liked.

While Surge was looking for a new sword, Denise figured she should find herself a weapon. Since she was now living with a group of bounty hunters, it only made sense for her to have a weapon of her own. She started by looking at pistols, which came in two main varieties, energy powered projectile weapons and multi-shot energy blasters. As she looked at the guns, she remembered Yuki's suggestion of her being a cowgirl for the Halloween party and she decided against getting a ranged weapon. She wanted to get a katana, but she felt it would be too similar to Surge's weapon.

She went to a bin containing several types of non-Japanese swords. She picked up a cutlass, thinking it would be a good weapon for her. After all, she had been dressed as a pirate for the party. Holding the steel blade in her hand, she noticed a pair of hook swords mixed in among the other blades. She put the cutlass back in its scabbard and tossed it aside in the bin. She picked up the two hook swords and determined that she was going to have them. She walked over to Surge, holding the two swords in her hands.

"Surge, can I get these?" She expected that it would take some convincing before he would let her get them.

"Sure, why not?" He answered without the slightest bit of resistance. After finding a katana he liked, he took all three swords to the shop owner.

"Would you like to change the color of the beam?" asked the owner. He flipped a switch on a sword and a yellow beam appeared between the tip of the hook and the top end of the crescent shaped guard.

"What color would you like it to be?" Surge asked.

She smiled. "Purple. My favorite color."

"All right, that will be 100,000 credits," said the shop owner.

They paid for their weapons and left the store. "Where are we going now?" Denise figured that they were not heading back to the *Crimson Blade*.

"Well, I was thinking-" Surge was interrupted by the ringing of his handheld. "Hold on, it's Ray."

Ray's face appeared above the round handheld computer that Surge pulled out of his pocket.

"SURGE! Who told you, you could spend 100,700 credits?!" yelled the thirteen-year-old, with an outraged look on his face.

"Relax, we made 3,000,000 credits," Surge said, trying to justify his spending. And he was getting tired of the kid genius yelling complaints.

"If I wasn't able to fix the physical and cyber damage caused by the pirates, you would be paying almost all of that for the repairs to B-10's synthetic organs and the total overhaul of the *Crimson Blade*'s systems!" Ray explained. "We need to-"

Surge turned off his handheld and put it in his pocket. "That took care of that," he stated, with a smirk, just before getting a text message from Ray.

He pulled the handheld back out and read the message aloud. "Great... *'Surge, If you don't come back soon I will send Kira to bring you back!'* Guess we're going back to the ship," he said, annoyed. He did not want to fight Kira.

As the two of them made their way to the ship, Surge received a message from an anonymous source about a bounty that paid 10,000,000 credits.

Karl awoke after a strange dream about becoming a nameless prince. He jumped up, disturbing the cat, and glanced over at the mass of metallic gold strands on the opposite pillow.

Sophia opened her eyes and raised her head. She climbed out of her bunk, put her shoes on, and refastened the chain around her waist. "I'm going to pick up my arm," said the alien. "Are you planning to stay in bed all day or are you coming with me?"

"Is there really a difference between day and night in space?" Karl asked, not expecting an answer. He stood up and ran his hand along the cat's back. "Guess it's time to eat, Lightening." Lightening's ears perked up and he jumped off the bunk.

Karl straightened his clothing and followed Sophia out the door.

"Attention all crew," said the captain's disembodied voice, as the three of them walked down the corridor. *"We are approaching an Aether storm. Be careful going down the halls. I don't want to hear any complaints about shock wounds."*

"Certainly a compassionate man," Karl said, with a sarcastic tone.

"Well, what do you expect of a pirate?" Sophia asked.

"Treasure, adventure, and endangered princesses," answered Karl.

"Food, food, and food," Lightening answered.

Sophia ignored the statements made by the males and forged ahead of them. A sudden jolt passed through the *Lady Eris*. Karl grabbed a railing to the left of him. Sophia lost her balance and attempted to grab the railing with her left hand, forgetting that the left arm had been detached. She shielded herself with her right arm as she hit the floor.

"You all right?" asked Karl.

"Maybe you should lend her a hand," said the cat.

Karl grabbed Sophia's right hand and pulled her to her feet. They returned to Gavin's machine shop where Sophia's repaired left arm occupied a tabletop. Gavin was nowhere to be found. Sophia walked over to the table and reattached the prosthetic arm. She moved the prosthetic around as though it was a real limb, then noticed a black wire wrapped around her wrist. She uncoiled the three foot long object and found that it was connected to the bottom of her left wrist.

"What did he do to my arm?" she asked, looking both confused and upset. She clenched her fist. The black wire extended from her arm like a rod with a curved end running into the bottom of her wrist.

Then the wire started to glow bright yellow. Immediately recognizing it as a plasma coil, she partly opened her hand and the wire wrapped itself around her wrist after returning to its dormant state. She walked off in search of Gavin, to have him explain the situation behind her arm's new weapon.

Karl was left behind and started looking at the stuff in Gavin's room. He noticed several orange crystal bolts encased in gold springs. The bolts were each about an inch long, and with the gold spring, they were roughly the size of .45 caliber bullets.

As Karl picked up one of the bolts, the door behind him slid open. He turned around to see Zrela standing in the doorway. "Where is that son of a belgrack?" She stood there in just a tank top and a pair of extremely short shorts.

"If you're talking about Gavin, he's not here," Karl answered. "And Sophia already took off after him."

"Well, that's a shame. I guess I'll see him later." She walked closer to Karl. "So, Mr. Sabers, I heard you were interested in Lecaran females." She wrapped her arms around his neck. "Is that right?"

His face turned red as her yellow lips approached his mouth.

"Karl, food time." The cat jumped on Karl's back, causing him to accidentally kiss the alien woman on the lips.

She stepped back with a surprised look on her face. "Well, that's the first time a Terran actually kissed me," said Zrela, touching her lips. Her look of surprise quickly turned into a wicked grin. "You really do have xenophilia don't you?"

"That's not true," Karl stated.

"How would you like to have some fun?" she asked. Without giving him a chance to say anything, she wrapped her arm around his neck and dragged him out of Gavin's workshop.

They walked down the corridor of the residential deck and went up to the dining hall for something to drink. The dining hall was large enough to accommodate eighty or so crew members. Across from a bar, on one end of the hall, was a black flag a the skull and crossed swords.

Karl and Zrela bypassed several mismatched chairs lined up at each of the four long tables. They approached the bar where three people were already sitting. The only one Karl had directly encountered before was his casino dueling partner, seated apart from the others, were two Terran crew members.

Reginia still necessarily retained the hated black armor and jacket worn by the aliens that attacked Karl's home. Karl knew she could not take it off. It was her only protection from the hotter temperature and heavier gravity of the spaceship.

But its visibility contributed to her isolation.

"Bartender, two shots of rum," Zrela demanded. A Terran man with long white hair tied in a braid walked out with a barrel of rum. He pulled out two small glasses and poured each of them a drink. "Drink up, Mr. Sabers." Zrela picked up her glass and drank it in one gulp.

Karl looked at the liquor in front of him.

Alcohol had been illegal on the *Nomad,* and even if it had been legal, he would have been underage. But he figured he was involved with pirates already, so drinking was not going to make his criminal record any worse.

He picked up the glass and took a sip of the rum.

Despite the fact that he had never taken a drink in his life, he actually enjoyed the taste. He then drank the rum in one swallow. The bartender pulled out two more glasses and filled them to the brim.

"Great, a drinking contest," said the cat. "This isn't going to end well. Bartender, I want a bowl of tuna juice."

Zrela drank another shot of rum and placed her second glass inside her first.

Karl was about to take a second drink when a violent jolt passed through the ship, causing him to spill his drink.

Zrela downed her glass with no problems at all.

"Can't hold your liquor," the cat commented.

"This coming from someone who can't hold anything," said Karl.

"Who needs hands when you've got slave labor?" Lightening asked, licking his paws.

The bartender refilled Karl's drink and he took another gulp.

The drinking continued until the bar became Zrela's pillow. Karl, on the other hand only felt a bit drowsy.

"Shouldn't I be drunker now?" Karl asked, looking at the snoring alien beside him.

"Zrela has a rather low tolerance to alcohol," said Reginia. She drank her water through the small hole in her helmet. "As for your ability to handle alcohol, old translator chips are known to have odd side effects. But keep drinking and you'll probably get drunk." Reginia slid her glass over to the bartender and walked off.

"And I'm sure having a cat rework your brain had nothing to do with it," said Lightening, as he got into Karl's lap and began rubbing his face against Karl's.

Karl took his hand off the glass and began stroking Lightening's back.

With Zrela now an immovable decoration for the bar, Karl decided to find something else to do.

He got out of his seat and Lightening climbed on his shoulder.

As they were about to leave the dining hall, members of *The Lady Eris'* crew poured into the dining hall, taking seats at the long tables.

Captain Gavorlo Micalo stood in front of the pirate flag with his first mate standing behind him.

They both had their hands placed behind their backs and gave off the aura of men prepared to meet their end.

"I guess they're preparing for a battle," Karl whispered to his cat.

"And it doesn't look like there will be any food involved," said Lightening.

"Why would there be food involved?" Karl asked.

"Well, as you know, I'm an optimist," the cat answered. "There is always a chance for food if people give off a happy scent."

The transparent image of a rectangular ship, with three broad cylinder shape engines coming out of the stern, appeared in front of the captain.

"This is the ship which shall be our next target," Micalo stated. It took Karl a few seconds to realize that the ship the captain was referring to was *The Starlight*. "This vessel is carrying slaves and large amounts of Kei. The captain has a habit of shanghaiing most of his men, so the crew won't likely put up much of a fight. In fact, we have a member of her crew right here." The pirate captain smirked and raised his hand towards Karl. "This is the man who is going to get us onto this ship," he said, as everyone looked at Karl.

Karl now understood why he had been forced to join the pirates.

The captain knew that Karl had his access codes for the *Starlight*, and would make capturing the ship a lot easier.

"Oh, great. That's what they wanted," Karl said under his breath.

"You were there when Sophia told you about this," Lightening reminded him. "But wait you're only a male human..."

"Now, bartender, drinks all around," said the smiling captain.

102

Chapter 13- Problems with the New Cook

The *Crimson Blade* landed in the hanger on a small lifeless rock that could hardly be called a planet.

She was one among many other small vessels, most of which had been converted into gunships for the purpose of bounty hunting and mercenary jobs.

"Looks like we're not the only ones here," Surge stated. "Seems like this job may be legit." Surge had a difficult time convincing Ray that the job was worth rushing the ship's maintenance.

With Ray manning the helm and B-10 still in need of repairs, Denise was given the job of shooting anything that wasn't Surge or Kira, should trouble break out.

Denise, Kira, and Surge walked down the ramp underneath the *Crimson Blade*. Denise would have preferred the option of trying out her hook swords, but instead they gave her an assault rifle with a sickle-shaped bayonet. They headed towards a crowd of mostly Terran bounty hunters with some Koal and Lecarans mixed in. Among the bounty hunters were a few people that Surge recognized, including a hooded woman with an eye patch and a rapier at her side, walking towards him.

"So you got the message too," said the woman.

"Yeah, got any idea what this is about?" asked Surge.

"No," she answered. "All I know is that some of the best bounty hunters and mercenaries in the galaxy are here."

"You don't think it could be a trap set by the pirates," said Kira. "It wouldn't surprise me if they were trying to eliminate a major threat."

"Rest assured that this job isn't some kind of trap," said a Lecaran man with silver hair and yellow eyes, wearing a white coat trimmed in gold.

Beside him were two other men. One was an old Lecaran with a thick black beard carrying a briefcase. The other was an armed figure with a three lens eyepiece on his left eye.

"I have summoned you here because you are the best of the best. I am Dergan Fafnir, and my job for you is very simple. I need you to bring me, dead or alive, a woman who is attempting to trigger a war which will bring destruction to both Lecarans and Terran alike."

The bounty hunters showed no reaction to his statement.

The older Lecaran opened the case and gave every group of bounty hunters a yellow gem.

"You're looking for a girl with gold hair and red eyes. Her blood type is one known by Terrans as L4. These stones will turn red when you have found her or a close relative of hers. Her body must be brought back with real genetic material. You will receive a payment of 1,000,000,000 imperial credits when a woman that reacts to the gem is brought to us and another when she is confirmed to be the one we seek. The last lead we had was in the Tau Ceti System, where she may have involved herself with pirates."

After his statement, the three Lecarans left the bounty hunters to their own conclusions.

As Surge, Kira, and Denise made their way back to the *Crimson Blade,* a group of three bounty hunters, which Surge and Kira both recognized, started walking towards them.

The leader was a blonde haired man in a black coat with a katana on his back. The second was a muscular man with tattoos running down his arms, and the third was a woman who looked almost exactly like B-10. They were one of the few groups of bounty hunters which the crew of the *Crimson Blade* was truly at odds with.

"Well, if it isn't the halfbreed and his pet," said the man in the black coat. "And I see you got a new servant."

"Srack," said Surge, gripping the hilt of his katana. "Shall we end things here?"

The blonde man seized the sword on his back.

"How many little girls will you need before that desire of yours is fulfilled?" he asked, referring to Denise's underdeveloped appearance.

"Take it back!" Denise yelled, pointing her gun at the man. At that moment, Kira grabbed both Denise's and Surge's arms and began dragging them back to the ship.

"Let me fight him, he has it coming!" Surge demanded, struggling against Kira's hold.

"Surge, you can play with your archrival later," said the Lrakian as Surge and Denise tried to get free. "Ray thinks we should leave as soon as we can."

They were brought onboard the *Crimson Blade* and lifted off the dead rock. As they got ready to travel through the Dark Space

Corridors, a gold and black frigate, several times larger than the *Crimson Blade,* appeared in their path. The bow of the long slender ship resembled a split arrow head. And connecting the twin cylindrical engines to the vessel's stern were a pair of rear swept wings.

"Looks like a vessel from the Neith Federation," said Ray, just before the ship slipped into a starless pocket of space. "Lay in a course for the Tau Ceti System, or head to the closest pirate haven?"

"Most of the bounty hunters will likely begin their search in the Tau Ceti System," Surge stated, sinking into his chair. "Lay in a course for the Dainare System, and then you can go back to fixing B-10. Kira, take a nap. Denise, have dinner ready soon."

"All right," Kira said, with a smile on her face.

Denise glared at Surge when she got her orders.

"That's what he bought you for," stated Ray. "Time to get our money's worth out of you. There should be a list of spice restrictions in the galley."

"Hurry up. I'm getting hungry," Surge said, smiling at her.

"All right, I'm going," she said, getting up from her seat and heading down the spiral staircase. *Well, this time I won't let him ruin his food like last time,* she thought. She made her way down the octagon shaped corridor.

She walked into the galley and decided to make spaghetti. Denise found the list Ray was talking about. The list mentioned several poisons which Ray and Surge requested not to be used to season their food. Denise thought it would have been idiotic to put that stuff on food anyway.

The oddity was the fact that any individual dish made for Kira contained large amounts of lead. She opened up the collapsible pots and started boiling the water and cooking the sauce. While the food cooked, she pulled out a folding table, cleaned it, and then placed a tablecloth on it for dinner.

After a few minutes, Surge, Kira, and Ray smelled the food and came to the kitchen. The males sat down and awaited their meal. Kira got plates and set the table, providing everyone with a double edged knife and a fork with three prongs arranged in the form of a triangle.

"How much longer is it going to be?" complained Surge, who continued to sit there, not doing anything.

105

"Just a few more minutes," Denise answered, as she put the spices in the sauce. She wanted to force Surge to help, but after seeing what he did with his food she knew that wouldn't be a good idea. When the food was done, she brought it to the table and joined the others.

Kira got herself a plate of spaghetti, and then pulled a small bag of gray powder lead out of her dress pocket. She carefully poured the powder on her food trying to make sure she didn't get one of the most essential minerals for her race into anyone else's food.

Surge looked at the spaghetti on his plate.

"This looks like it would be good with some caramel, chili, and peanut butter," he commented killing Denise's appetite.

Great! Just what I needed. Denise thought to herself, as the mental image of all the food mixed together turned her stomach.

She got up from the table and found a container. Putting her share of the food in the fridge, she decided she would just come back later that evening when Surge wasn't around. Noticing the person who made her lose her appetite get up, she turned and watched as Surge began collecting the ingredients that he mentioned a moment ago.

"Don't you dare!" Denise said, pulling a knife from the silverware dispenser, causing the bounty hunter to freeze. "Put the peanut butter back, and eat your food like a human being."

"But I'm a halfbreed!" he stated, trying to convince her that there was nothing wrong with the way he ate. He didn't like the way she was holding that knife to him.

"You're half human, so half of you is going to eat like one, even if I have to cut the alien half out!" The knife had a dangerous gleam to it, which matched the wielder's eyes.

"You better listen," said Ray, who didn't really approve of the way Surge ate because of financial reasons. "Women are the most dangerous beings in the universe. The Martian Imperial forces still haven't been able to reconquer the Republic of Aihtycs since it declared independence in 3590."

Surge surrendered the peanut butter to the five-feet, one-inch tall girl with the knife. Denise may not have been an Amazon super soldier, but she had the personality to become one.

The two of them went back to the table despite the fact that Denise had no plans to eat anything.

After eating, the others left Denise to clean up. While it was something she would have complained about doing, she felt cleaning the kitchen was a small price for preventing the creation of whatever Surge would have made.

She looked around for a few minutes before finding small cans of cleaner that were about the size of a roll of quarters. Holographic writing which appeared around the cans provided her with directions on how to use the cleaner. She pressed down on the top of the can and a green spray came from the bottom of the can covering the counter.

Within five minutes, the green chemical evaporated leaving a surface she could see her reflection in. She proceeded to clean the entire kitchen with that substance.

Onboard the *Lady Eris*, Karl waited in his cabin with Lightening. The crew had locked him in his quarters on the basis that he might try and help the *Starlight* in battle.

Except for Alice, there was no one among the *Starlight*'s crew that he really got along with. The crew didn't even need to interrogate him to get the security codes to access the *Starlight's* systems.

As he waited in the room, the door slid open and the Koal woman, Reginia, came in the cabin, carrying a tray of food.

"Your third harem alien has arrived," said Lightening, jumping off the bed. "And she brought lunch!"

"So, what are you doing here?" Karl asked the alien, who was still encased in her armor.

"Bringing you food," she stated.

"I mean why are you not raiding the *Starlight?*" he asked, hoping for something that would strike a conversation.

"My skills in zero gravity combat were not needed," she answered.

"So they left you behind," he stated as he picked up his cat.

"You may look at it that way if you wish," she said. "The battle should not last long and your companion will return."

"By the way, what do your people look like under that black armor?" Karl asked, just before Lightening bit his neck. "Ow."

She left the room without answering his question. "Must be a personal thing," Lightening commented. "I wonder how many more alien girls you'll have before your Xenofetish is satisfied."

"Are you going to start that, too?" Karl asked, glaring at the cat.

"I won't if you feed me," Lightening answered.

Giving into his demands, Karl gave Lightening a portion of the meat in his meal.

"Look at it this way, if you keep giving me your food, you won't have to worry about getting fat again."

"I hope Alice is all right," said Karl, remembering that he had told Sophia to be on the lookout for the Terran girl.

"Are you sure she knows what you're talking about?" asked the cat. "Don't worry about it, your job is to sit and wait while the pirates fight."

The crew onboard the *Starlight* saw, appearing in a flash of light, the cylinder shaped pirate ship with three engines arranged in a triangular form. The ship quickly overtook the rectangular cargo vessel.

A series of green pulses came from the broadside of the *Lady Eris* and struck the *Starlight's* hull.

The *Starlight* returned fire from a pair of mini railguns which fired their projectiles like machine guns. A volley of seeker missiles was launched from the *Lady Eris*.

The majority aimed straight for the *Starlight's* guns while two of the warheads flew right by the cargo ship.

While the rapid fire quickly eliminated the main warheads, another two missiles curved around and obliterated the *Starlight's* weapons.

A series of cables were fired at the cargo ship, followed by the activation of the pirate ship's tractor beams. The two ships were dragged towards each other. Several transparent floating skulls were projected in several areas within the *Starlight*.

"This is Gavorlo Micalo, Captain of the Lady Eris," said all the skulls at once. *"Unless you surrender your ship and cargo, I will personally drag your souls into the Abyss."*

Within moments of Micalo's speech, the crew of the *Lady Eris* began boarding the *Starlight*. Both crews fought primarily with melee weapons, because almost any range weapon powerful enough to penetrate a personal shield was likely to damage major systems or penetrate a ship's hull, much like firing a pistol into the hull of a wooden vessel.

A thin glowing, bright yellow rod cut a circle in the ceiling, then slid upward, and the cutout circle of metal dropped to the floor. Two Lecaran pirates dropped down from the glowing red circle.

The first was Sophia, dressed in a black dress and her trademark glass heels. The other was the taller copper haired Zrela, wearing a tank top and long pants. Standing in front of them was a dark brown skinned Terran female armed with a plasma knife.

"Die, pirate!" exclaimed Alice, before switching on her weapon.

A glowing purple blade of plasma extended to its maximum length of two feet.

She charged at the Lecarans.

Sophia clenched her fist and the loose coil around her wrist extended into a glowing yellow blade. Yellow and purple clashed as the Lecaran blocked the Terran's weapon.

Alice jumped back. Sophia slashed with the blade on her left arm. Alice dodged the swing. Sophia attempted to stab Alice in the side. The Terran girl deflected Sophia's blade upwards and kicked the Lecaran in the stomach.

Sophia staggered back. Unconsciously, Sophia relaxed her left hand, causing her weapon to revert to its bracelet form. Alice saw her chance to dispose of the Lecaran woman. She rushed at Sophia.

Sophia moved out the way and grabbed Alice's wrist joint with her mechanical hand. She squeezed Alice's hand until Alice dropped the plasma knife. Then Sophia threw the Terran girl against the wall.

Sophia dusted off her dress, then picked up Alice's deactivated plasma knife. Alice slowly stood back up.

"You want to keep going?" asked Sophia, while pointing the Terran's weapon at her. "If not, you can go waltz over to the escape pods."

"You're just going to let me go?" Alice asked, surprised.

"Do you want to die for honor or something like that?" asked Sophia. "If you'd rather walk out an airlock you can."

"I'm going." Alice staggered over to an escape pod.

"I'm surprised you just let her go," said Zrela. "Most would have killed a Terran adversary on the spot."

"Well, Karl saved my life." Sophia dusted her dress off. "So I guess-"

The Terran girl turned back to the Lecarans. "Karl?" Alice asked, interrupting Sophia's statement. "Are you by any chance talking about Karl Sabers?"

Sophia then recognized the dirty Terran as the girl that she ran into at the store.

"You're that friend of Karl's that I ran into right after he bought me," she stated. "If you had said something, I wouldn't have had to hurt you."

"Where is Karl?" she asked.

"We left him on the ship," answered Zrela. "The captain doesn't trust him enough to let him leave."

"I can capture you and let you see him again if that's what you want," offered Sophia, with a sarcastic tone in her voice.

"Or we could just have her join the crew?" suggested Zrela.

"All right, I'll come with you," said Alice, taking the Lecaran's offer. "So long as I can remain in space."

As an immigrant worker within the Titan Empire, Alice would likely be sent back to Jupiter's moon, Europa, once the loss of the *Starlight* was made official. If that happened, it would be unlikely that she would ever be able to travel the stars again.

Shortly after the three girls met, the crew returned to the *Lady Eris* with loot and prisoners. Among a half dozen captured were Jacob, Justin, and Alice. However, the only actual hostages were the two from the *Nomad*.

It was a frequent occurrence for those turning pirate to claim they were forced to join, and rare for people like Karl and Sophia to actually be forced into piracy.

The crew assembled in the dining hall after inducting the new members. Karl was allowed out of his cabin, then left to meet with Sophia and his friend from the *Starlight*.

Karl found Sophia at the bar drinking with a bruised Alice.

"Looks like they're now drinking buddies," said the cat. "Well, onto more important things, what are we about to eat?"

"Hi, Karl," said the Lecaran woman. "I brought your friend back, though we had a bit of a misunderstanding."

"Karl, may I ask how you ended up as a pirate?" asked Alice, who wasn't too happy about being slammed into a wall by Karl's former slave. "I have a feeling that this misunderstanding might not have happened, had you not made that career change."

At that point, Karl was aware that Alice knew about him selling out the *Starlight*. Now he had the problem of what do since the blame had been shifted to him. Karl slowly began to move away from the girls.

"Well, it wasn't exactly my choice to become a pirate," he stated, trying to avoid more trouble.

"Did your alien companion somehow force you to join the pirates?" asked Alice, while glaring at Sophia. "Aliens are prone to taking things that don't belong to them."

Sophia crossed her arms. "I'll let that comment slide because I already gave you a beating," she stated, glaring at the Terran girl with her ruby red eyes. "But if you keep making comments like that, I'll find out how much pressure it takes to crush a Terran's upper spine."

Sophia picked up her metal cup with her hand, consumed the liquid and wadded it into a ball with her cybernetic fingers.

That night Denise slept in her bed, which Ray had lowered to accommodate someone of her height. As she slept there, she was awoken by the sound of her door sliding open. In a daze, she groaned and pulled the covers over her head to block the light of the corridor. Becoming more awake, she heard the footsteps of a person entering the room.

"Kira, I thought you said this room was mine now," Denise said, thinking the catgirl was returning to her old territory.

Denise felt a hand touch her leg through the sheet. She instinctively kicked the hand and rose up, keeping the sheet covering her legs.

"Denise," said the voice of Surge. "I love you."

"WHAT?!" she yelled, not knowing how to react and not exactly sure what was going on. This was the first time that a guy, who wasn't related to her, had ever said that to her.

"Li-li-Lights on!" Kira's swimming fish reappeared on the walls of the quarters, as Denise saw the drowsy looking Surge standing there in his boxers.

"Surge, w-what are you doing here?" she asked, holding the sheet closer to her body.

"What are any of us doing here?" he asked, holding his right hand off to the side.

"Surge, are you all right?" she asked, looking at him warily, thinking he might be drunk or something.

"Never felt better," he said, turning to face the wall as if that's where she was.

Before Denise had a chance to say anything, the door slid open again. Both Kira and Ray came in the room dressed in their pajamas.

"What's going on?" asked Ray.

"I should be asking that!" Denise stated, pointing to Surge. "Is he drunk or something? Get him out of here!"

"He never touches any mind-altering drugs," Ray answered. "It's most likely that one of his enemies poisoned him. The question is how? It wasn't his food because my brilliance has remained intact."

The young teenage boy stood there silently in thought for several minutes.

"Something smells like window cleaner," said Kira, smelling the cleaner Denise had used to clean the kitchen. "You used a chemical spray, didn't you?"

The Lrakian glared at Denise as though she had committed some kind of great offense.

"So, I don't see the problem," stated Denise. "What does the chemical spray have to do with anything?"

"It's common knowledge," Ray said, crossing his arms and closing his eye. "Just as we Terrans receive adverse effects from ingesting certain chemicals, Lecarans receive negative effects from certain chemicals they inhale, many of which affect the functions of the Lecaran's brain. Surge inherited negative qualities from both his parents."

"Indeed I did," stated Surge with a proud tone in his voice. "All of their weaknesses and none of their strengths." Surge turned to Ray and placed his hands on the boy's shoulders. "You'll have to forgive Danielle, she's completely ignorant and lacks the basic intelligence to survive in the big bad galaxy."

"Ignorant and lacking intelligence?!" Denise repeated, shouting. She stood on the bed, forgetting she was only in a large shirt with no pants. "You call me an idiot and you don't even have the decency to remember my name!"

Jumping off the bed, she picked up a shoe and hit Surge over the head with it. The bounty hunter dropped on the floor, promptly passing out.

"Do all adult Terrans sleep in their underwear?" asked Kira.

Denise, realizing what she had done, grabbed her sheet and crouched under it in the fetal position.

"Everyone, get out!" she yelled, hiding under the sheet. She couldn't believe this was happening.

"Don't let me grow up to be like them," said Ray to Kira.

"Don't worry I won't," Kira replied, patting Ray on the shoulder.

"Everyone out right now!" Denise yelled, popping out from under the sheet to throw her other shoe at them. Kira quickly left with Ray in tow.

Denise threw the sheet over Surge as he sprawled on the floor. She pulled on her pants before sticking her head out the door.

"Come back in," she demanded.

Ray and Kira returned as Surge began to stir on the floor.

"Why do we even have that stuff onboard if it makes him sick? And can we get the guy a robe?" Now fully dressed, Denise averted her gaze from Surge, looking at Ray and Kira.

"We have to clean the place every once in a while," said the boy. "But chemical cleaners are to be used only when Surge is not onboard."

"So, how long is he going to be like this?" she asked, daring a peek under the sheet at the intoxicated Surge. "Also, why wasn't I given any rule book or anything? I've never been around Lecarans."

"Surge will likely be this way until the cleaner is completely filtered out of the ship," Ray answered. "If the cleaner was left in the air for several days, Surge would eventually go completely insane and die a slow painful death. However, the filtering process should only take half a day at the most. Oh, and Surge was supposed to have given you one, so blame him for that."

Surge crawled out from under the sheet and gazed at the ceiling.

"Twelve hours of this," Denise said, with a gloomy countenance as the three of them watched as Surge started playing with one of the hanging cat toys.

Chapter 14- Return to the Pink Planet

Having captured, looted, and hidden the *Starlight*, the *Lady Eris*, under the command of Captain Micalo, rendezvoused with Ashley Claymore on Dainare III.

Using an assumed name, the pirate ship landed in the same hanger where Karl had docked the *Devil's Fang* over a month before.

The pirates began unloading their loot and transported it to Claymore's shop on the planet.

The loot consisted mostly of rare spices which would fetch a pretty penny for the band of thieves.

Karl was surprised that it was not the same cargo of slaves that been there when he was onboard.

After transportation of the cargo was complete the crew assembled at a local inn, celebrating of their victory over the small cargo ship.

The pirates drank and ate their fill as the money from the sale of the stolen cargo was divided among them.

A generous 90,000 thousand credits were paid to each of the pirates who participated in the battle.

Karl received a mere 10,000 for handing over the codes to the *Starlight*.

Once nearly everyone was in a drunken sleep or with a companion, Karl left the building with Lightening tagging along as usual.

Not wanting to be left behind, Sophia chased after them.

"Where are you heading?" asked the alien girl.

"I want to get one of those personal shields," Karl answered, figuring his sword was going to be his most effective weapon when fighting onboard a ship.

He should at least have something to protect himself from any firearms that couldn't penetrate a ship's hull.

Karl remembered shooting that Lecaran thug with a pistol and the bullet just shattered.

"Wonder why the Koal who attacked the *Nomad* never used them?"

"Classic case of the villain's stupidity outweighing that of the hero," said the cat. "When do we eat?"

"We just did that," said Karl.

The three of them came across an arms store and went inside.

The walls were lined with glass cases that housed a multitude of different ranged and edged weapons.

Just in front of the force field covering the back end of the shop were several small glass cases with items that looked like jewelry.

Sophia walked over to the jewelry cases while Karl started looking at the weapons.

He thought buying a new pistol might not be a bad idea, since he didn't have much ammunition for the .45 auto.

But, as he looked, he discovered that most of the more powerful handguns were out of his price range.

The only weapon he was willing to spend his money on was a small derringer-like energy pistol.

"Karl, I think I found what you were looking for," Sophia stated, calling Karl over to the section she was looking at.

Most of the jewelry was either a small shield device or some kind of concealed weapon.

The object that seemed most appealing to Karl was an object labeled "light buckler", which looked like a thick brass knuckle with a large round piece of glass mounted in the center.

Karl hit a button which called forth the shop owner.

A Koal in his black armor and coat came out from the back of the store and looked at the two of them through the forcefield.

"What can I get you?" asked the alien hidden by a black helmet.

"I'm interested in that derringer," Karl answered, thinking of using the small pistol as a backup weapon to keep under his sleeve. "And could you tell me about the light buckler?"

"Well, on standard setting it works like your basic personal shield," the Koal answered. "But it also produces a forcefield that ripples away from the crystal, which is powerful enough to stop glass weapons with a charge-cutter that comes within a foot of the crystal. The two of them together will come to 20,000."

"Which do you think I should get?" Karl asked his two companions.

"So long as it doesn't come out of my food money," answered the cat. "You'll probably need both of them, considering the trouble you're about to run into."

115

He got no answer from Sophia, who was looking at a diamond shaped crystal brooch with a silver back.

"I want that one," she said, pointing at the personal shield generator of her choice.

"She's paying for that one," Karl said to the store owner.

Sophia put the brooch on her dress directly over her heart. "How does it look?"

"It looks nice," Karl said, figuring it was the best answer whether he cared or not.

He walked out of the store and headed back to the hanger where the *Lady Eris* and the *Devil's Fang* were docked. He was once again followed by the cat and the Lecaran. He turned around and looked at both of them. "I understand why the cat is following me, but why are you following me?"

"Well, I have nowhere else to go," she answered, not looking directly at Karl. "Everyone else is drunk or involved with something else."

"In other words, she's afraid of being alone," Lightening stated.

Sophia's face turned bright yellow. "That's not true!" She tried to strategize. There had to be a way to counter the cat's comment. But she wasn't able to come up with anything at the time.

She stayed quiet until they got to the hanger.

They walked onto a lift, which took them down to the level housing the *Devil's Fang*. Karl returned to his stolen ship and paid the overdue charges on the small attack vessel.

Karl was considering the idea of abandoning the pirates and asking Sophia if she wanted to join him. Perhaps he could get his sister back and try to find the *Nomad* as well as the other students taken from the Academy.

"So, you have your own ship," Sophia stated, while walking up behind him. "Where did you get her? Most people your age wouldn't be capable of buying a small space vessel like this."

"He stole her from his fellow refugees onboard the ship that attacked the *Nomad*," Lightening answered, while perching on Karl's shoulder. "His first act of piracy."

"So, you were a pirate before even meeting Captain Micalo," she commented. "I'm surprised you weren't ecstatic over the idea of joining a pirate crew."

"I did it to rescue my sister," said Karl, trying to justify his act of piracy.

"You have a sister?" she asked, as they started walking back towards the lift. "You never mentioned her before. Where is she now?"

"She was sold as an indentured servant to a bounty hunter before I was able to get her back," Karl answered, feeling as though he was admitting to failure. "So I was planning on working something out with this bounty hunter or, if necessary, waiting until after her time's up and then taking her back."

"Then you got involved with an alien girl who has led you into nothing but trouble," said the long hair tabby. He rubbed his face against Karl's neck.

"What was that, cat?" Sophia asked, glaring at the yellow-orange feline.

"Your girlfriend seems to know nothing about showing respect to her superiors," said Lightening, stepping off Karl's shoulder. "Looks like that trouble is here." Lightening walked along the catwalk and disappeared from sight.

A figure in white armor walked up to Karl and Sophia, carrying an assault rifle on its back. In its hand was a yellow gem which turned dark red when it approached them. Without saying a word, the white figure grabbed Sophia's right arm and started dragging her away.

The wire wrapped around her left wrist uncoiled itself and took the shape of a gun in her hand.

She pointed the tip of the wire at the figure's head.

"Let go," she commanded.

The figure did not comply with her order. A yellow blast came from the end of the wire and destroyed the figure's head. The figure released its grip and staggered back, but did not fall.

Another killer robot?! Karl thought, as he reached for his khopesh. *Why the hell do I have to fight another one?*

Before he had a chance to draw his weapon, Sophia grabbed his right hand and dragged him along as she ran away.

He reached into his pocket with his left hand and pulled out his new light buckler. *This thing better work!*

The robot pulled its assault rifle from its back and released a spray of glowing metal bolts as Karl and Sophia turned a corner on the catwalk.

Fortunately for the two of them, the personal shield generators were doing their job.

Seeing that its weapon wasn't powerful enough to penetrate the force fields surrounding them, the robot tossed the rifle aside.

The machine's chest plate split open, revealing several pencil-sized missiles, which were then launched at Karl and Sophia.

Karl stepped in front of Sophia and blocked the missiles coming at them with his light buckler.

Sophia fired two shots at the robot's open chest.

The machine dropped to the ground with a small red hole in its torso.

"You two make a decent pair," said a man with dark goggles over his eyes. He walked down a flight of stairs. "Too bad I'll have to break you up."

"And you would be?" asked Karl.

"The one who is going to collect the money for capturing that woman," he answered, pointing to Sophia. "But if you hand over that Lecaran, I'll let you live."

"Sounds like I've heard that before," Karl stated, pulling his .45 from his jacket.

Sophia pointed her built-in weapon at the man. "What would be the point of capturing me?"

"Money, of course," the bounty hunter answered.

He snapped his fingers and three more of the white humanoid robots came down the stairs behind him and stood in front of him.

Sophia opened fire on the enemies in front of them, as the machines advanced.

Much like the Koal armor, the white plates covering the robots were able to absorb energy shots making Sophia's gun useless.

Karl fired two shots at one of the robots, cracking the robot's covering but not doing any real damage.

"Time to go," said Karl, as the two of them started running away.

One of the robots jumped in front them, blocking their path.

Karl quickly put his gun back in his jacket, then drew his khopesh and activated the glass blade which turned orange with the charge-cutter field's activation.

Two energy blades shot from the robot's wrists, and it ran at Karl

118

as the other two went for Sophia.

A purple beam made a diagonal pass through the robot in front of Karl, melting the torso section of the machine.

Karl looked down to see Henry Hunter standing on one of the lower levels holding a long rifle with a disk shaped scope.

A Lecaran man dropped down from above them and landed between Sophia and the robots.

Karl recognized the man as Ellris, who was carrying a halberd with a yellow glass blade. He sliced the machine in half with the weapon's axe head and stabbed the other in the chest.

After seeing his machines fail him, the bounty hunter took off running. The slash of an edged weapon was all that was heard after the bounty hunter disappeared from sight.

A few seconds later, Calidi came down the stairs with a red version of Ellris' weapon.

"Looks like the other pirates are better fighters than you," said Lightening, who had returned from his hiding place.

"Coward," Sophia said, glaring at the cat.

"Hey, I have to conserve my remaining lives as best I can," Lightening said, rubbing against Karl's leg. "Robots are hard to knock down."

Ellris turned to Calidi. "Master, I think we should inform the captain it's time to leave."

"Correct assessment," Calidi replied.

Karl's handheld rang. He pulled the round object out of his pocket.

"You guys all right?" asked Henry's voice over the handheld.

"Yeah, we're fine," Karl answered. "So, how did you find us?"

"Well, Ellris and Calidi told the captain that it would be a good idea to make sure you didn't run off," he answered. "And the captain said to back them up."

"That's trust for you," Lightening commented.

"So, the captain forced you to miss out on drinking with your buddies to come watch us," Sophia stated.

"Well, I'm actually a teetotaler," Henry said.

The next day, the hungover crew of the *Lady Eris* left Dainare III after restocking the ship's supplies to avoid trouble with more bounty hunters.

A bluish-white flash streaked from bow to stern as the pirate ship vanished from the Dainare system.

"Well, thanks to that encounter with bounty hunters we've had to leave the Dainare System," said the blonde haired man who acted as the first mate. "Since we picked up Karl Sabers and those two from the lost colonies, bounty hunters have gone after us in a pirate haven. On top of that, Claymore wants us to go retrieve even more of these lost primitives."

"What do you propose we do, Mr. Long?" asked the pirate captain, Micalo, with his arms crossed. "Dump them on the closest planet, and waste the valuable data leading to the other lost colonist from old Earth?"

"I have a better plan," Mr. Long stated. "One that should present us with a fine profit."

"Aye, Wilhelm," Micalo replied with a smirk on his face. "I think I understand what you have in mind. I guess it was about time we cut our ties with Claymore anyway. I'll trust you to make the necessary arrangements."

The captain walked over to his chair and pressed a button on the armrest.

"Attention all crew, set course for the High Chapel of Ralethim."

A few hours later the *Crimson Blade* emerged from dark space covered in a blackish-red film, which peeled away revealing her crimson hull.

"Sir, we have arrived in the Dainare System," B-10 stated, having returned to her former station on the ship after being repaired by Ray.

"Don't shout like that," Surge stated, placing his hand on his forehead, still having the hangover-like effects of the cleaner. "Land us on the planet."

Without saying a word, she landed the ship in the same hanger the *Lady Eris* left earlier that day.

As the crew of the *Crimson Blade* left their small ship, they saw the caped cops carrying a body on a stretcher.

"Wonder what happened?" Denise asked, wearing her hook swords on the back of her belt in the form of an X.

"I'll check it out," Surge stated, before walking towards the cops.

He had previous experience with these cops and knew he could get information out of them.

"Well, if isn't Surge," said the younger cop, swishing his cape. "How have you been?"

"So who is this?" asked the bounty hunter. "May I take a look before we have a game of cards?"

"I don't think that would be a problem," said the older cop.

After confirming that the corpse belonged to another bounty hunter who had also been at the meeting held by Fafnir, Surge and Ray sat down with the cops for a game.

"Have any ideas why he died?" asked Surge, shuffling the deck of cards.

"Not really," said the older cop as the cards were dealt.

"Most likely hunting pirates," the younger officer commented. He picked up and looked at his cards. "Which is pretty stupid considering the governor's take on things. 'If it didn't happen here, it's not our problem, and if it happened here, we'll eventually look into it'."

"I don't even know why you bounty hunters come," said the old cop.

"Oh, something interesting that I heard," said the young cop, dropping three of his cards. "Around the same time that guy was killed, a couple consisting of a Lecaran woman and a Terran man was seen entering this place followed by a cat."

"A cat?" asked Surge.

"A fur covered quadropod from Old Earth," Ray stated, drawing two cards. "They went extinct from an alien virus brought over during the invasion of Earth, then mysteriously reappeared a decade after the invasion of Earth in both Lecaran and Terran varieties."

"I know what a cat is," Surge stated, looking at his cards. "I was just wondering what the cat had to do with things."

"Probably nothing," said the older cop, placing his hand down revealing his three jacks. "Three of a kind."

"I got nothing," said the younger officer, folding.

"Full house," Surge stated with a smile on his face, revealing his three aces and two queens. "I guess I win."

"Flush," Ray said, unveiling his hand of cards with only hearts. "I win."

"Beaten by a kid," said the older cop, throwing his cards down.

121

"It happens to the best of us," Surge commented, reshuffling the cards. "So heard anything else interesting lately?"

"Not much," said the older officer. "Members of the Syndicate are keeping pretty quiet and the freelance pirates are just selling their stolen goods, getting drunk, and sailing off."

"That dead bounty hunter is the most excitement we've had in months," said the younger officer. "But I do remember someone saying not too long ago that there was some kind of power struggle for control of the Syndicate."

While the males spent their time talking and playing cards, the girls went shopping on the planet.

"Where do you want to go first?" asked Denise.

"I think we should buy you some dresses for your dates with Surge," Kira answered, walking into a clothing shop close by.

"I'm not going on any dates with that man!" Denise protested, with her face turning red. "B-10, don't we have more important things to buy?" she asked, looking for a way out of dress shopping with Kira.

"I am sorry, but I will have to side with Kira," B-10 stated, ending Denise's hopes of escape. "I have to replace the clothes damaged by Thorn."

Denise let out a depressed sigh and followed the others into the store where she quickly became Kira's dress-up doll.

Denise was forced to try on dozens of different outfits until the alien catgirl was satisfied, including an Ancient Japanese sailor style school girl uniform, a puffy princess dress, and a maid costume.

Kira left the store wearing the sailor uniform while carrying the other clothes. After buying clothes she found practical to fight in, B-10 left the store.

She was followed by Denise, who had bought an outfit she felt suited a bounty hunter. A pair of black cargo pants, combat boots, a red tank top, with a pair of fingerless gloves and a black jacket.

They rejoined Surge and Ray in the hanger and made preparations to leave the pink planet.

"The High Chapel of Ralethim is one of the holiest places of Evlon faith." Sophia perched on her bunk. She wore just a long-sleeved pajama top and pair of shorts. "A Terran religion that appeared after the invasion of Earth."

Karl had no knowledge of Evlon and the task fell to Sophia to explain things to him. "They believe that no two races could have evolved so similarly to each other. The founders of Evlon concluded that the Lecarans and the Koal were unnatural. So, they came up with the idea that another race was jealous and created both the Koal and the Lecarans as a mockery of the Terran race." She slapped her forehead with her right hand and tilted her head down. "I can't believe I just said that. I think I'm going to be sick."

"So, we'll be traveling outside the Titan Empire?" Karl asked.

"Well, Evlon is the only sect to openly threaten the Vatican and the Titan Monarchy," she answered. "And, with the exception of a few Jovian states, it is almost entirely banned within the orbit of Sol. I can't understand why he would risk an encounter with the High Chapel. No warship of the Neith Empire was ever able to penetrate the shields surrounding that place."

"A man and woman alone in a room together just to talk about religion," said Lightening, scratching his ear with his back paw. "How disappointing. Well, time for breakfast."

Sophia grabbed a red blouse and a black skirt before leaving for the women's shower. Karl pulled out a new suit and left for the men's showers.

Afterwards the three met in the dining hall of the ship where they ate breakfast.

Karl's meal consisted of grilled fish, rice, and miso soup while Sophia had a creature that looked like a blue reptile with four claws and a beak.

Lightening had bacon.

They were soon joined by Zrela, Alice, and Henry, also wanting food.

"How're you guys doing?" asked Henry.

"Fine," Karl answered. "So, why exactly are we headed to this Shrine of Ramham?"

123

"The High Chapel of Ralethim," said Alice, correcting him. "I don't know but-"

"The captain isn't crazy enough to attack that place," said Zrela, taking a drink. "There's no way a small ship like this could get beyond Aegis."

"The Aegis?" Karl asked. "From Greek Mythology."

"The shield that surrounds the High Chapel," said Alice, eating her order of eggs.

"The Sargoth of the Neith Empire sent an entire fleet to attack Ralethim fifteen years ago. Every ship was destroyed by the power of the station," Sophia stated, causing Calidi and Ellris who were sitting not too far from them, to take notice of the conversation

"I heard that was because the fleet failed to starve the chapel into submission before a sympathetic fleet of ships from Io arrived," Alice stated, taking another drink.

"No, I was on one of the ships from Io that came to defend the High Chapel," said Henry. "When we got there, every enemy ship had been destroyed, but we were told to keep the events of what we saw there a secret under pain of death. How did you know about the events of the battle?" Henry looked at Sophia.

"Even I didn't know that the fleet was destroyed by a single battle station until Henry told me a few years ago," said Zrela, pouring herself another drink. "And I've studied the history of Neith pretty thoroughly."

"I don't know," Sophia said, holding up her right hand and showing the slave bracelet embedded in her wrist. "I can't remember anything about myself beyond the point when Karl bought me."

The two Lecarans got up from their seats and walked towards them. "Only the Sargoth's Court and members of the royal family knew of the events that happened," said Calidi, standing over them. "I wouldn't think many Lecarans outside the Federation government would know about that since most of the Sargoth's advisers and the royal family are dead."

"I thought there was one princess who survived," Karl said, remembering what Sophia told him about the Neith Royal family.

Ellris' purple eyes widened in reaction to Karl's statement.

"Sounds like you said something that's about to cause trouble," said the cat.

"Karl, I think you should recheck your information," said Alice. "It's a well known fact that the Sargoth, his wife, and their nine children were executed by a firing squad at the end of the Neith Revolution."

"Vlora was not executed with the royal family," Sophia stated, with her arms crossed. "Of that I am certain."

"What makes you confident of that?" asked Zrela. "If I remember right, you just said you didn't remember anything about yourself."

Sophia remained silent while trying to think of an answer. The average process for sealing memory was something that only stopped a person from remembering past events about themselves, but left necessary knowledge and specialized skills intact.

"That's enough," said Calidi. "If the girl believes what she said, then your correction will be in vain."

Feeling that she had been insulted, Sophia put down her eating utensil and walked away. Karl followed her and Lightening finished what was left of Karl's food before chasing after them. Karl didn't have a real justifiable reason for following the girl, but still he did. He followed her through the gray corridor of the ship. As she turned the corner, Karl turned as well and crashed into what felt like a thick sheet of glass. Karl was thrown backward and landed on his back.

"Sophia!" he called out. Sophia kept going without even noticing him and made another turn, disappearing from sight.

"Looks like someone is trying to separate you," said Lightening.

"Looks like it," Karl stated while standing back up. "I wonder what's going on."

Karl started wandering the ship with the cat until he came to the cargohold. There he found the location where Justin and Jacob were being kept in a cell consisting of a corner wall and a bent force field to act as the other corner. The area Justin and Jacob had been placed in was not much smaller than the cabin they had shared with Karl onboard the *Starlight*. The cell was angled in such a way that anyone who walked in the cargohold would see anything they were doing. Karl quickly took notice of Reginia, who had been given guard duty. The black armored alien sat in her chair, with her handheld in her left hand and her thin sword at her side.

"Well, if it isn't the traitor," said Justin.

Traitor, huh? Karl thought, trying to restrain his anger. "And

125

would you be calling me a traitor because I ended up with a pirate crew or because I work with aliens?" Karl asked.

"Both, of course," said Jacob.

"Half of this crew consists of the same aliens that conquered Earth," said Justin, glaring at Karl. "And on top of it, this woman is a Koal herself. You should be-" He was cut off when Reginia ceased the flow of sound through the forcefield.

"Sorry," said Reginia, looking at the series of colored shapes being projected from her handheld. "But this noise is interfering with my reading."

"You should thank her," said the cat.

"What are you doing here?" asked Reginia, not bothering to look up at him.

"He got separated from Sophia and got lost while looking for her," Lightening answered.

"I did not," Karl stated.

"You did too," said the cat, licking the area between his legs.

"Attention, Reginia," said the voice of Micalo from over the Koal's handheld. "Secure the three prisoners, and bring them to Longboat B."

Three? Before Karl even had a chance to turn around, the tip of Regina's black sword was against his neck. "Why do these things keep happening to me?" Karl asked.

"At least she hasn't knocked you out yet," said the cat.

"I guess that's a plus," Karl stated, as Reginia removed his sword.

After taking the derringer Karl had in his pocket, Reginia led Justin and Jacob out of their cell and escorted the Terrans towards the *Lady Eris'* hanger deck. Not surprisingly, Karl's antique .45 pistol remained undetected beneath his waistcoat. However, the weapon would likely be useless against the pirates, who each carried a personal shield.

Karl walked through the gray corridor knowing that this was probably the last he would see of this ship. Calidi and Ellris stood in a doorway smirking at the Terrans as they walked by. When they arrived, they entered a large room with a pit area that held three long cigar shaped vessels which Karl assumed to be the longboats. The captain and his first mate stood by the starboard hatch of the longboat. The three were forced into the small transport, which had two long benches one each side of the hull. Sitting on the portside, he found Henry Hunter dressed in silver and black armor with a helmet sitting beside him. In his hands was a shorter version of his rifle with a curved, serrated bayonet on the end of the barrel. Micalo followed them before the hatch closed, with Reginia and Mr. Long staying behind.

The three young men lounged there with grim faces. "No need to look so depressed," said Micalo, looking at them with his red eyes. "The place you are going to will treat you very well. You may not ever have to work again."

"Look on the bright side," said Henry. "You won't be a wanted criminal anymore."

Karl looked out the window and saw a long vertical metal cylinder with several smaller parallel cylinders connected to it by bridges. The object grew larger as they came closer. Two silver fighters came from the top cylinder and escorted the longboat on either side. Between the nose and pilots was a long thin gun twice the length of the fighter's cockpit. On each side of the cockpit was a weapon with three prongs around it, and extending from behind the pilot's seat were two angled rods attached to a pair of small triangular engines. The fighters guided them towards a docking bay, and a beam pulled the longboat in. The doors to the docking area closed and a gangplank extended from the wall.

"Time to get going," said the captain, pointing a pistol at Karl, Jacob, and Justin. Henry placed an eyeless silver helmet over his head as the hatch opened. Two old men in blue robes appeared at the other side of the gangplank, one of which had a long white beard and the other was a bald man with a limp. At that point, Micalo and his armored crewman began escorting the three men from the *Nomad* down the plank.

"I wonder if the food is any good?" said Lightening, riding on Karl's shoulder.

"I don't think that's what we should be concerned with right now," Karl whispered back.

"You're just upset because all your alien girlfriends are on the pirate ship."

"What alien girlfriends?" Karl asked. "Don't tell me you're going to keep making Xenofetish comments."

"Sophia, Zrela, Alice, and Reginia," said Lightening, nuzzling his face against Karl's neck. "I would count Yuki in the harem, but she hasn't made an appearance since the invasion."

"Alice and Yuki aren't aliens," Karl said, trying to correct his cat.

"Terrans, Lecarans, Koal, you're all aliens as far as I'm concerned," Lightening said, lumping all sworn enemies into the same category.

When Karl reached the end of the gangplank, he took notice of the metal objects which went around the back of the old men's heads and the five pointed stars on the center of the old men's robes. Each star had a red, black, white, brown, and yellow point with Earth at its center.

"Are these them?" the bearded old man asked Micalo.

"Yes," he answered, looking both men in the eye. "Do you have the payment?"

The bearded old man pulled a thick gold disk with a large crystal in its center from his robes. He handed it to the pirate captain.

"These three are worth more than a map to nothing," said the other man. "Take your prize and leave."

Micalo took the disk and held it in front of Henry. "It's safe," Henry confirmed with one glance. Micalo placed the disk inside his coat and the two pirates turned around, returning to the longboat.

Karl considered making some kind of a scene but it would have been a pointless effort. Karl was now accustomed to being moved around against his will. If the people from lost colonies were as valuable as this man made them out to be, these people might help him get his sister back ahead of her release date.

"Welcome, honored guests," said the bearded man. "I am High Theorist Kordova. Allow me to escort you to the quarters we have prepared for you." The three of them followed Kordova into a large elevator and were transported to another section of the station.

The longboat quickly began to slide out of the docking bay. When the longboat was halfway between the High Chapel and *Lady Eris* four missiles were launched from the station. The first warhead struck the longboat and detonated within the small vessel consuming every molecule of oxygen in a single explosion that left only the smoking hull of the longboat drifting in space. The second and third were struck by the *Lady Eris'* starboard ray guns and the fourth hit its mark, destroying one of the ship's stern engines and tearing a large hole in her metal hull. A temporary forcefield prevented the pirates from being sucked into the vacuum of space.

As a second volley of missiles was launched at the *Lady Eris* as a bright flash streaked across the hull of the pirate ship. The *Lady Eris* vanished, forcing the missiles to disarm and return to their launching tubes.

Meanwhile, Karl and the other Terrans followed Kordova down the wide curved corridors of the station, unaware of the battle outside. Karl looked at the iron statues which lined the gray corridor, beginning with an image which resembled some kind of rodent, and progressed through into different types of apes until taking on the form of humans. His sister would have pitched a fit over the statues glorifying evolution. The scene of his sister kicking the humanoid statue in the stomach and causing the others to collapse in a domino fashion quickly entered his mind.

The group stopped at a door which was slightly darker than the wall.

"This is where you will be staying for the time being," said Kordova, as the door slid open, leading into a room not too dissimilar to the dorms in the Galaxy Academy. "Rest up, the High Council will wish to meet with you shortly." Kordova left the former students to themselves.

After a day's rest, Karl, Justin, and Jacob each changed into a set of white clothes, consisting of pants, a pullover shirt, and a thin jacket. Kordova returned to escort them to the High Council's chambers, where they were seated along the inner rim of a table with the shape of a crescent moon. Five members of the High Council entered the room wearing similar robes to Kordova with the same head device. The councilors took their seats on the outer edge of the table.

"It is an honor to meet with you," said an elderly man with the councilors. "I am Dabid Euroce, I trust that your journey was not an unpleasant one."

"Tell me, how did you three manage to come into existence without our knowing of it?" said a beardless old man who appeared to be the most aged of the council. "You aren't clone agents sent by the

Lecarans?"

"No, Jozaf, the scans have already indicated that they are the real thing," said a bald withered old person, who they had believed to be a man until they heard her speak. "I say we ask them where they come from."

The youngest man on the council turned to them. "Well then, where do you come from and how did you come into the possession of pirates?"

"To begin, we're from the *Nomad*," said Justin, having already decided to trust the people in front of him. "During the invasion of Earth, the orbital platform that was home to my ancestors departed Earth. Our journey continued until we came under attack by the Koal. After which, my peers and I were captured by the Koal."

Karl froze, not knowing what to say or do in this situation.

Once the council had been informed of everything that had happened after they were taken from the *Nomad*, they were permitted to leave the council chamber.

Kordova was placed in charge of giving them a tour through the High Chapel. "So what have you learned concerning events of the after-invasion?" asked Kordova.

"The Lecarans ruled by the Ruby Eyed Empress were the ones who sent the Koal to Earth," Justin answered. "The humans, living aboard orbital platforms, converted their applications into generation ships and left the solar system. Then at some point after, the Titan Empire and the Mars Imperium were formed by those who remained."

"Lecarans and the Koal are responsible for the fragmented state of humanity," stated Kordova. "The empire came into being because Caesar Nicolas I admired the monarchy of his Lecaran conquerors. The Titans and Martians mimicking of the Lecarans is a blasphemy that will someday be corrected."

"What is so blasphemous about an imperial monarchy?" Karl asked, not seeing the idea of divided humanity as something which clashed with any kind of scripture he had read or heard about.

"The Lecarans and Koal were merely things created as copies of humanity," Kordova answered, instructing them in Evlon doctrine. "The Greys which observed Earth for countless ages, created the Koal as a way of having stronger servants to do things their lesser counterparts could not. The Rlacs created the creatures now known as

Lrakians. And the sworn enemy of the Elders, formed the Lecarans as a rival to the human race. Identical in build and construct to us, an act which could only be defined as plagiarism."

"Who are the Elders?" asked Justin.

"Some kind of ancient alien that they think humanity is the heir to," whispered the cat. "Just like the Ancients, Forerunners, Old Ones, and Protoculture in fiction."

Sounds too farfetched to me, Karl thought to himself.

"Come along." Kordova continued down the hall. "While no bodies of the Elders have ever been recovered," he explained, as they came to a large set of white double doors, which opened up as they drew closer, "we have discovered relics of their technology on several worlds."

"This is sounding more like fantasy every minute," Lightening whispered to Karl, as they walked down the bridge to another hall. "I will never understand the desires of you humans, and your need to make things up when you encounter something you don't understand."

They followed Kordova to an elevator which took them up several floors to a room resembling a small chapel constructed out of metal. In place of a cross, hovering over a glass altar was a globe of the Earth, and images showing the stages of evolution took the place of stain glass windows. Sitting on the glass altar was a disk which looked almost exactly like the one Kordova had given to Micalo.

"Greetings, Oracle," Kordova said. He walked over to the altar and knelt before it. "I have brought unto you-"

"Three men born in isolation from the galaxy," said a deep voice which echoed through the room, as the disk lifted itself into the air. Two clear gems extended from the top and bottom of the disk and four others extended from a groove running around the edge of the disk.

"Yes, Oracle," Kordova replied. "What-?"

"Their fate is uncertain." The Oracle answered Kordova's question before he had a chance to finish it. "Their destiny has yet to sow itself into the temporal lines. You may bring them to me again when I call for it."

The Oracle retracted the gems and landed back on the altar.

They left the small chapel and made their way to what Kordova called 'The Grand Altar Room'. As they walked down the next hall,

Karl tried to understand everything that was going on. From what he saw, the Oracle was an alien device they discovered or something this cult had built and decided to worship. As they walked along, they saw people wearing white garments with the same head device as Kordova. The people in white made their way to another large set of double doors, beyond which was an amphitheater that towered twenty stories. Hovering above the floor was a silver sphere which acted as a screen, repeating the same image which could be seen from every angle.

Once the tour concluded, the three of them were free to travel throughout the station as they pleased. After they had split off, Karl received a call from a message from an unknown source,

"Do not trust the followers of Evlon. If you wish to regain your freedom come to the chapel of the Great Oracle. A friend will be there to greet you."

"So you're just going to blindly walk into another situation where you have no idea what's going on?" Lightening stated, rubbing his face against Karl's hair. "Like that has worked the last half dozen times you tried it."

Karl stopped to think about the situation he was rushing into. Realizing that he had left his antique pistol, he returned to his room to retrieve it and changed back into his brown suit which was better constructed to conceal his gun.

He then headed to the chapel, trying his best to avoid getting captured again. As he approached the chapel, Karl sent Lightening through to see if the coast was clear.

"See anything?" Karl asked, ready to draw his pistol.

"Just the black guy with the huge rifle," said the cat.

Karl looked over and saw a still-armored Henry standing beside the altar. "Was it you who called me down here?" Henry asked.

"Didn't you return to the ship with the captain?" Karl asked. "I thought you were in the longboat with him."

"The captain's dead," Henry informed him. "They destroyed our Longboat right after you left. If you didn't-" His statement was interrupted by a blackout within the chamber.

They both turned to the Oracle Disc as it rose from its altar. The gems extended from all sides once again. "It was I who called you both here," said the Oracle with his deep voice. "The task appointed to you is-"

"Feed me lunch," Lightening interrupted, looking at the disk as though it were a plate of food.

"Feed the cat lunch," said the Oracle. Within seconds, the gems turned yellow. "What! No, that's not right!" The disk stated losing its deep and regal tone. "Oh, great." The Oracle turned blue, after realizing what had just happened.

"What's going on?" Karl asked. *He was just putting on an act?* "Lightening, what do you think?"

"To have tuna? To have ham?" Lightening said, giving his thoughts. "That is the question."

Great, should have expected that, Karl thought to himself.

"So, what was it you called us for?" Henry asked, pointing his rifle at the Oracle. "And what does it pay?"

"Wait! There's no need for that!" said the panicking object, its voice no longer as controlled as before. "You guys want to get back to your ship, right! I can help! Stop pointing that at me."

"We're listening," Karl stated, as Henry lowered his rifle. "What's the catch?" Karl was thinking that he should start being a little more suspicious of people.

"I want out of here," said the disc, as its crystals turned orange. "I want to see the universe. There has to be more to the stars than just the data I've looked at. Also, these people are convinced that I'm some sort of messenger from their ancient ancestors."

"Well, aren't you?" asked Henry.

"How should I know?" said the Oracle. "My first memories were of when archaeologists discovered me in a ruined outpost on Severus V. Anyway, I've shut down the security sensors in this area. So they can't hear us. From this area you can take the main elevator shaft, cross over to the main spire, then you should be able to grab a couple of fighters in the hanger and take off."

"What about you?" Karl asked. "I thought your plan was to get out of this place."

"It is," said the Oracle. "I need you to take my container with you. Once we're passed the Aegis shield, I'll be free to move on my own, and delete all the information about us from their systems."

The disc closed up and Karl took it from the altar.

Henry pulled out a long pistol with a curved bayonet on the end, and a face mask with large lenses.

"Be sure to put that on in case a shot pierces a hole in the outer wall of this place," he stated. "On the low setting, it should be powerful enough to get through most personal shields."

They made their way to the elevator just as the Oracle instructed.

"Hey, Karl, you could live a life of luxury as one of them. Why would you choose to leave that behind?" asked Henry.

"He just wants to get back to his love interest," said Lightening, as the elevator moved downward.

"Because I don't like the way these people operate," Karl said, giving a partly true answer. One of his main reasons for wanting to return to a life of crime was because he missed Sophia.

"So your Xenofetish is really that bad," said Henry.

"I fail to see how being friends with a female Lecaran makes me have a weird fetish," Karl commented.

The elevator door slid open and led into a large hanger with fighters floating between the piers, extending from a series of interconnecting bridges. Most of the fighters were round pods with three blade-like wings, except the two silver fighters that had escorted their longboat. Both fighters had their wing pods retracted making them resemble lances.

Karl walked towards one of the silver fighters and opened the canopy. Henry hit the panel to open the canopy of another fighter.

"Karl, get ready for a fight," Henry said, pulling out his rifle.

They heard the sound of a screeching alarm which caused several white robed figures to appear on the bridges. In their hands were metal staffs, which began firing red bolts of energy. Henry squeezed the trigger and dragged a beam across the line of priests. A few of the shots came at Karl from above. He drew the pistol Henry gave him and fired two green shots at his enemies.

One of them fell, landing on the hanger level beside Henry.

Karl and Lightening jumped in the cockpit, which had two controls for each hand, both equipped with a trigger and a hand-grip lever. Lightening hit one of the four buttons near his left. The silver canopy closed. The console around the rim of the cockpit lit up.

Karl looked down at the floor of the cockpit and saw a curved monitor beneath the six pedals which depicted everything below the fighter. He stepped on the top right pedal, and the fighter made a vertical ascent slamming into the triple winged pods above.

"Why is that one up?" Karl asked, looking down at the pedals. He stepped on the top left pedal, thinking that it would cause the fighter to descend. The Lancer then crashed into the dock to the left of him, knocking several of the priests to the floor. "Who came up with this thing?"

"Someone who played too many video games," Lightening commented.

All right, six pedals, six directions, Karl thought, before slowly pressing on the bottom right pedal, which caused the fighter to move away from the dock. He looked down and saw Henry toss a glowing sphere at the back end of the other Lancer, before jumping into one of the triple winged vessels.

The Lancer fighter exploded in a ball of green flames.

"Karl, follow me," Henry commanded, as his face appeared in a small window on Karl's monitor. Henry's fighter flew towards the closed doors at the bottom of the hanger and began firing from each of the three pulse guns located between each of the pod's wings.

Karl squeezed the two triggers on his controls, firing two sets of red beams from the claw-like guns just under the cockpit. Their efforts had little effect and only scarred the doors blocking their way.

"I'd prefer if you'd not waste one of my lives like this," Lightening said, placing his paw on one of the buttons of Karl's left controller.

The red beams stopped firing, and the large gun that formed the nose of the fighter lit up with bolts of purple lightning. Four seconds later a thick purple beam shot from the nose, melting a hole in the doors large enough for them to escape.

"I'll be expecting a reward for this."

"Worry about food later," Karl said, flying his fighter out of the space station.

The station began launching missiles at the two pirates. "All right we're passed the shield," the Oracle said, coming back online. "How's it going?"

"Look outside!" Karl yelled.

The Oracle took notice of the missiles coming at the fighter. "Oh. Just a second," the Oracle said, as bright flashes streaked across both fighters, sending them into another area of space.

"Karl, are you still there?" asked Henry.

"Yes," Karl replied, before he realized what had happened.

The Oracle was now completely inactive and the two fighters were in orbit below a gray planet.

"Do you know where we are?"

"Yes," Henry said, looking up at the graveyard-like planet above them. "It's Reharal, an abandoned colony world. Now it's just the location of a pirate port. I think if the *Lady Eris* was able to escape, and she was damaged in the fight, she would probably be here. But-"

"But, what?" Karl asked, not liking the last word of Henry's statement.

"It should have taken us several weeks to limp here using just the flash drives in the Lancer," he explained. "But according to the clock in my helmet, only three days have passed."

"Wait! Three days just passed?" Karl asked.

"Let's see, at three meals a day, that comes to nine meals that you owe me," Lightening stated. "I would like payments made in beef, pork, and chicken. Turkey is not acceptable."

"We better head to the port, then get out of here as quickly as possible," Henry stated, with a sense of urgency in his voice. If what he knew was correct, the Elvon priests were not likely to let the pirates off easy.

The engines on the Lancer extended from the fighter along two rod-like wings and the craft sped off towards the pirate haven with Henry's pod following close behind.

On the other side of the planet, the battle-scarred *Lady Eris* occupied one of the twenty docks extending from a largely abandoned station, which had long since broken from its orbital elevator.

The entire crew was in an uproar over who would become the next captain.

Seeing this as a distraction and her chance to leave, Sophia gathered her belongings. With Karl's sword on her left hip and the strap of her bag on her left shoulder, she floated across the tube which acted as a gangplank between the ship and the station.

She had no desire to stay with the people who sold off Karl to

Evlon, and she was not willing to be purged with them if the temple priests showed up.

Her basic plan was to find someone willing to take her back to Dainare where she would take possession of the *Devil's Fang.*

As she made her way towards the entrance of the station, three shady looking men dressed in suits with flat caps floated by her.

They were led by a hooded Lecaran woman in a purple cloak.

Sophia was convinced that the scoundrels were only a foreshadow of the future for the pirates.

She stepped down. She began tapping her glass heel against the metal floor as the artificial gravity took effect.

What had once been the security gates of the port had become a threshold of gambling and black market trades.

Sophia felt her weight increase pound by pound as she entered the dirty enclosed town.

She entered a tavern in search of a place to stay the night and find someone willing to take her to Dainare.

She walked up to the hardwood bar where a male Lrakian with a cat-like tail was serving drinks to the outlaws lining the bar.

"Well, how are you doing, young lady?" asked the furry-eared bartender, as Sophia walked up to the counter.

"I want a room and information on the cheapest way out of this system," she stated. She pulled out a round handheld computer with her left hand.

"That will be 2,500 for the room," said the bartender. "I don't know of anyone who would take passengers for less than 800,000."

Sophia knew she could buy her own ship for the price he just mentioned.

And she figured there was no way she could legally come up with the money.

She paid for the room and made her way to the staircase which led up to rooms on the next floor.

As she ascended the flight of stairs, an old cyborg with a mechanical right arm and leg started walking towards her.

"Hey, princess. I've been feeling a bit lonely," he said, reaching out to her with his metal hand. "How about we spend some time? I pay well."

"I'm not interested," she said, walking up the stairs.

She went to the room and slipped the long triangular key into the door.

The door slid open and she walked in, with the door closing behind her.

She changed out of her clothes, leaving them neatly folded in a chair, and climbed into bed.

She awoke to the pressure of a metal leg pressing down on her left arm and opened her eyes to find herself staring down the barrel of a one inch gun.

She recognized her assailant as the same cyborg who tried to chat her up the night before.

"So are you a slave trader, or a bounty hunter?" she asked. "Either way, my master isn't here."

"You think I'm interested in that small time ship jumper?" he asked, taking her question as an insult. "Bringing him in wouldn't even pay for the trip here."

"Guess, I couldn't be that lucky," Sophia commented under her breath.

She had hoped that she wasn't his target.

The harsh reality that her life had been in danger from the moment Karl had awakened her meant that she was undoubtedly a threat to someone.

"So what am I wanted for? Titan law says you have to tell a criminal what they're charged with."

"But the people who put a price on your head aren't Terrans," he answered, with a smile. "So, I don't have to tell you anything."

She quickly pulled Karl's plasma derringer from under her pillow and fired two shots at the man.

The energy pulses dissipated upon hitting his personal shield.

He grabbed her right arm with his human right hand and squeezed her right wrist until she dropped the gun.

"Maybe I should just kill you now," he said, moving his gun over her heart. "All I need is a body. I'm sure they won't mind too much."

"Being used as a bloodhound plot device isn't my idea of a good time," said a familiar voice from beyond the closed door.

"Well, would you like to be replaced with a real bloodhound?" asked another voice.

"How do you know they even still exist?"

"Okay, I'll get some kind of liz-" The door slid open to reveal Karl standing there looking into the room.

"Looks like we came at a wrong time," said the cat.

Karl and Lightening took cover just before the bounty hunter fired his massive pistol, destroying the wall on the other side of the door.

Her attacker was distracted by Karl. Sophia saw her chance.

The wire around her left wrist changed into an energy blade.

She attacked.

Before he even realized it, the bounty hunter lost the front half of his metal leg.

The bounty hunter fell on his back just before the wire curved around Sophia's hand to form a gun. Karl reentered the room, pointing his energy pistol at the bounty hunter.

"You may have beaten me, but I will return to avenge me," said the bounty hunter, seeing both Karl and Sophia pointing their guns at him. "Remember the name, Berry Lane."

With that, he bit down on a tooth and died from ingesting poison.

"I wonder how he plans to avenge himself," said Lightening.

"Sorry I'm late," Karl said, looking at Sophia as she covered her lavender nightgown with a white sheet.

"Close the door," Sophia instructed.

She got out of bed and began examining the body of the bounty hunter.

Sophia reached inside a pocket on the corpse's leather jacket and pulled out a yellow gem. It glowed red in her hand.

She pocketed the gem, turned around and looked at Karl.

Seeing her glass shoe upside down on the ground, he picked it up, still curious as to how Sophia functioned with them. He then noticed that the sides and top of the shoe were made of flexible transparent fibers, and there was some kind of hinge built into the sole that allowed it to bend.

"Give me back my shoe," she demanded.

Having been trained by Denise to instantly obey such commands from mad females, Karl quickly complied with her orders.

"How did you get away?"

"He and a surviving pirate stole a couple of fighters," Lightening stated scratching his ear.

139

"Grab the clothes on the chair," she said, pulling a long coat out of her bag. She pulled the coat over her nightgown, just before grabbing it and the sickle sword. "We have to leave. Now!"

She opened a window in the back of the room and stormed down the escape ramp.

Karl followed behind her.

"You stole a fighter from the Evlon. I was worried they would be coming here to finish off the pirates, and thanks to you they will be."

She slipped her glass shoes on as she went down the ramp.

"Sorry, but what should I have done?" Karl asked, taking back his sword.

"So your only option was to commit an act of piracy against a religion that demands the death of all non-Terran humanoids!"

"This coming from the woman who took part in the capturing of a ship," Lightening stated, referring to the attack on the *Starlight*. "Hypocritical talk is not going to make you very likable."

"Can you two stop arguing?" Karl stated, looking at the alien and the cat. "Why was that guy after you anyway?"

She pulled out the glowing gem from her pocket.

"This is a Lecaran device meant to locate a member of a particular bloodline," she answered, as she put the gem back in her pocket. "Which means someone in my genetic family has a rather large bounty on their head."

"I think we should go back to the lost princess theory," Karl suggested, as they continued on down the back alley. "You said yourself that a member of the royal family would have the highest bounty in the universe."

"I would prefer that to not be the case," she stated, knowing that would mean she had inherited the legacy of a family with the blood of over a billion Terrans and Lecarans on their hands. "Let's get going."

"I don't think so," said another bounty hunter, who appeared before them.

This one was bearing the face of the last hunter. Unlike his predecessor, he lacked the mechanical parts, and he looked almost ten years younger.

He was armed with a silver carbine, which he proceeded to aim at Sophia.

With no hesitation, Sophia fired a one inch round from her new gun into the bounty hunter's torso.

"As I was saying, I'll be collecting the prize on that head of yours." This time, a still younger incarnation of the bounty hunter appeared behind Karl with a rifle pointed at the young pirate.

"What are you?" Karl asked.

"A repeated man," Sophia commented, altering the wire into the form of a gun. "A series of clones connected through a subspace cyber-link. I heard the Neith Empire scrapped the project a century ago."

"What a well informed young lady," he commented.

A screech came from Karl's handheld.

"Karl, we've got trouble!" Henry stated.

"I know. Bounty hunters."

"NO! Blood Terrans!" he yelled, sending a streak of terror in both Sophia and the bounty hunter.

"What?" Karl asked.

"No vampires, please," Lightening commented.

"No bounty's worth taking on Blood Terrans." The bounty hunter, lowered his gun, and left them.

The two of them stood in silence for a few moments before Karl turned to Sophia.

"How dangerous are these guys?"

"Well, they are the reason that Mars only has one moon," she answered. "They share similar viewpoints with the Evlon religion, that all non-Terran humanoids must be destroyed."

"Things just keep getting better and better," Lightening commented.

"So what's the plan?" Karl asked into his handheld.

"I don't know," Henry's voice replied. "They've completely blockaded the port and... dictate... Lan..." The pirate's voice was replaced by static.

"What now?" Karl asked.

"How much room is in your fighter?" Sophia asked, with a look of panic.

"It's large enough for Karl and me," Lightening replied. "We might be able to squeeze you in. I'll be nice and let you have the lap and I'll take the shoulders."

"Attention!" said a voice over the station's intercom system. "To

141

the pirate, Karl Sabers. This is Helen Anders of Blood Terra. You will surrender the item which you have stolen or face the same retribution as those who have infected Earth."

Surge sighed, looking at Ray. "I can't believe we're going to be stuck on this bubblegum rock."

"There are worse places to end up than Dainare III," Ray replied. "Besides, among the Terrans, pink is a masculine color."

"What?" asked Denise Sabers, coming down from the ship's gangplank. "Pink is a girl's color. Blue is the color of men."

"That hasn't been true since the invasion of Earth," Ray corrected. "The colors of pink and blue were only switched between genders during a brief period following the late 1800s. As a general rule, pink being a variation of red is associated with the color of Terran blood. Blue, on the other hand, is associated with the Virgin Mary and thus represents purity."

"Great," Surge let out. "The church dictating color."

"How dare you!" Denise cried, taking Surge's comment as an insult to her faith. "Mary gave birth to Jesus, the greatest Being to ever walk the wor-"

Denise paused for a minute realizing that neither she nor likely the two males in front of her had ever been to Earth.

"Any world."

"Denise, you don't need to take everything so seriously," the half alien commented.

"Surge," said Ray, before Denise could respond. "Might I remind you that I am also a Christian?"

"You are!" Denise exclaimed in happy amazement.

"Don't you start, too," Surge stated, just wanting the conversation to end. "It doesn't matter what the color of the planet is or what meaning it has. I don't want to be here."

Chapter 17- Inquisitor

A ship almost twice the size of the *Lady Eris* was now docked with the station.

Numerous Terrans, dressed in blood red uniforms, began sweeping through the station.

They knew that the station would be destroyed without a second thought.

The Terran majority occupying the station surrendered without a fight.

"The access hatch should be somewhere around here," Karl stated, as he and Sophia headed down towards where the Lancer was hidden.

"You haven't lost it, have you,?" Lightening asked.

"No," Karl answered.

Sophia said nothing. But her worried look quickly became one of panic.

"Here it is." Lightening stood on top of a metal hatch that was slightly thicker than the rest of the floor tiles.

They slipped in through the square panel and made their way into the under workings of the space station.

As they fled through the corridor lined with pipes and flashing fiberoptic wires, a figure appeared before them.

Its head was covered by a white helmet and body by a blue cloak draping from a pair of large pauldrons on each shoulder.

"Objective, secure the traitor to mankind," said the figure.

He spread out his cape revealing a suit of power armor. His armor was far bulkier than that of the Koal and in his right hand was the hilt of a bladeless sword.

A long slender rod with a triangular tip extended from the center of the grip.

Upon seeing the pentagram with the Earth at its center on his chest plate, Sophia immediately recognized the figure as an Elvon Inquisitor.

She raised the hand cannon that she had taken from Berry Lane and aimed at the figure firing a one inch shell at the armored warrior.

The round exploded on impact engulfing the armored figure in a fireball.

The figure then emerged from the smoke, pulling off his burning cloak as he slowly approached the two of them.

Karl quickly drew his pistol, ready to shoot. Sophia fired another round before grabbing Karl's arm, pulling him away.

A pair of red beams streaked from the hilt of the sword to the triangular tip as the Inquisitor charged at them. Karl and Sophia were unable to outrun the mechanically powered cuisses of the armored figure.

"Look out!" Lightening yelled. He then hid in an air duct.

Sophia's wrist coil unwound itself and was coated in glowing yellow plasma to block the red energy sword.

The Inquisitor kicked the alien girl in the side, slamming her into the wall.

The hand cannon dropped out of Sophia's left hand and was crushed under the armored figure's metal boot.

As the Inquisitor turned towards Karl, a burst of green plasma fired from his pistol struck the white helmet.

The armored figure staggered back, unable to see. Karl activated the charge-cutter on his khopesh and slashed the warrior.

Unlike his previous use of the weapon, Karl's orange blade was slow to sink into the chest plate of his enemy.

The Inquisitor kneed Karl in the torso knocking him back.

The enemy's now blackened and partly melted visor was quickly discarded, revealing the brown human eyes of the Inquisitor

"A worthless traitor and an alien thought they could get the best of me," he said, with rage filled eyes.

Karl pushed himself up, using his deactivated sword as a crutch.

"Now then-" The Inquisitor was suddenly interrupted by an explosion striking his back.

The armored figure turned to see a woman with long black hair and silver eyes coming towards him holding a rocket launcher.

"I cannot allow you to claim my master's target," the woman said in a monotone. "Please step aside or I will be forced to fire again."

"Mechanical wench." The Inquisitor charged at the android with his energy sword.

Another warhead was fired at the armored Terran who raised his left arm to block the rocket.

144

He swung his weapon and the android attempted to leap over the warrior with inhuman speed, but one of the red beams severed the machine's leg.

The synthetic humanoid tried to crawl away.

But her remaining leg was then crushed by the boot of the Inquisitor, who also rammed the metal tip of his sword through her forehead.

The Inquisitor was forced to abandon his twitching left gauntlet, before turning to find Karl and Sophia gone.

As he dragged the unconscious Sophia away from the Inquisitor, Karl collapsed from the pain of his wound.

The sound of strange humming came from inside his coat and the golden disc rolled out of his pocket.

Four crystals once again extended from the Oracle's rim as it floated into the air.

"Did I miss anything?" asked the Oracle. The floating object tilted towards Sophia. "Oh, is that a Lecaran? I've never seen one before!"

"Do something! Don't just float there," said the cat. "If you don't fix them you'll wind up as scrap metal."

"I don't think I was intended for medical function," the Oracle replied.

Lightening glared at the miniature flying saucer.

"But I'll see what I can find out." The Oracle's crystals turned to an olive green. "Let's see, there are a couple of broken ribs on the male and some internal bleeding on the female."

The crystals stopped orbiting the rim of the Oracle and pointed directly at the two wounded humanoids before firing a series of multicolored beams into the wounds of Karl and Sophia.

"Karl," said Lightening. He nuzzled Karl's neck. "Time to wake up. I forbid you from dying before-"

"What?" Karl awoke and immediately cringed at the returning pain of his injury. "Is Sophia okay?"

"Well, I closed her wounds," said the Oracle. "So she won't die of internal bleeding."

"We're going to have the same problem again," Lightening exclaimed. "If we don't get out of here now!"

Karl picked up the unconscious Sophia and took off running again.

"Did we win?" Sophia asked struggling to breathe.

"No," Lightening answered. "Karl took off as soon as the robot girl showed up."

The trio paused.

Just then, another figure appeared slowly from the shadows.

An unarmored man in a long coat gripped the hilt of what looked like a katana.

"So you have already encountered one of my comrades," the figure said, igniting a beam of flaming green plasma from the hilt of his weapon. "That's a shame. Good androids are hard to come by, but I assure you that the bounty will be mine."

Not another one, Karl thought, looking at the bounty hunter now revealing himself to be a blonde-haired Terran in a black coat.

Karl glanced over at Sophia.

"Will my sword work against that?"

"It should," she answered.

"I would think he would leave like the last guy," Lightening commented. "Considering the Inquisitor."

"I'm not going to let some fanatic get in the way of 1,000,000,000," said the bounty hunter.

"We'll just have to kill you before them." A larger, more muscular man stepped down the corridor behind the blonde bounty hunter carrying a large metal axe.

Lightening glanced over at the Oracle. "Okay, your turn," said the feline.

"Auhmm…" The Oracle paused for a moment. "I can't harm organics."

"What?!"

"My base program will not allow me to harm living creatures."

The cutting edge of the larger man's axe turned orange as though it was heated by a fire and the two bounty hunters charged at them.

Karl quickly activated the charge-cutter on his blade and the two orange weapons clashed against each other.

Karl drew the light buckler from his pocket to deflect another swing of the battleaxe.

The blonde bounty hunter swung his energy sword at the Lecaran

146

girl.

She attempted to block it with her wrist blade but was unable to stop the progression of the green plasma.

The green blade slid down against the yellow one as it glanced Sophia's forearm, burning away the synthetic flesh from her mechanical arm leaving the black metal exposed.

She kicked the bounty hunter with the sharp toe of her glass shoe.

The blonde bounty hunter staggered back, clutching his left side, before coming at Sophia again with his flaming blade of plasma.

Mere inches away, a single blast of plasma came from Sophia's damaged weapon striking the right wrist of the bounty hunter.

As the inactive energy sword fell to the ground, she kicked the bounty hunter in the stomach with a glass heel.

Sophia slid her foot under the energy sword's hilt and kicked it up into her right hand.

She ignited the plasma blade and rammed it into the back of the muscular fighter, while he was still engaged in battle with Karl.

The bounty hunter dropped his axe and collapsed on the floor in front of Karl.

"Can we get going now?" Lightening asked, standing on top of the blonde bounty hunter's body. "I'm sure you guys would rather get out of here before that Inquisitor shows up again."

Karl picked up the heat axe.

Sophia rewrapped the now disabled plasma coil around her damaged arm, before moving on.

"What now?" asked Karl.

"I don't know," Sophia replied, "Much as it pains me, I guess our best hope is to steal another ship and-"

Sophia was interrupted by the clanking of metal boots coming from behind them.

They turned to see another Inquisitor standing behind them.

Knowing that they could not outrun him, they turned to face their enemy.

"Halt!" the Oracle commanded. "Cease your combat once you're in the presence of an Elder-"

The Inquisitor stopped and began looking around at the others. "And where is it?!" demanded the Inquisitor.

The Oracle disk began to wobble for a few moments before

tilting towards Lightening. "This is the master race that took humanity under its wing."

"Thank you, Oracle," Lightening said, sitting there proudly. "Now as you did in Ancient Egypt, you can start building us pyramids again, if you like. But make sure they are housed with wonderful things such as fish, beef, steak and whatever delicious cat food can be provided in this age."

"You think you can fool me with a false Oracle?!"

The Inquisitor came at Sophia with his red energy blade.

Sophia knocked back her enemy's blade with the bounty hunter's green blade.

Karl came at the Inquisitor with the battleaxe, hoping that it would cut deeper than his own weapon.

The Inquisitor grabbed the handle of the battleaxe just below the blade and knocked Karl back against the wall before flipping the axe over and swinging the weapon at Karl.

The Oracle disk jumped between the glowing axe and Karl.

The head of the axe shattered in an instant.

However, the metal shaft still struck the edge of the floating disk sending the Oracle spinning in the air like a coin.

"Sophia, stop," Lightening commanded, as Sophia attempted to aid Karl. "He needs to handle things himself. You won't always be there to save him."

The armored figure raised Karl up by his neck.

"This is where you die, Xeno-lover," the Inquisitor said, ready to crush Karl's throat.

Struggling for breath Karl reached inside his coat and drew his .45 automatic.

With his right thumb, he drew back the exposed hammer of his pistol, then fired the gun three times point blank into the open section of the Inquisitor's helmet.

"That definitely counts as you getting knocked out again," Lightening stated.

Karl slowly opened his eyes.

Karl found himself resting in an unfamiliar room. "What happened?" he asked, raising himself up to look around the room. "Besides the getting knocked out part."

He immediately began looking for Sophia, but she was absent from this place.

"Well, there's good news and bad news," Lightening replied, sitting down on Karl's lap. "Which one do you want first?"

The door slid open before Lightening could say anything else.

In the corner of his left eye, Karl saw the apparition of the Ruby Eyed Empress with a dark armored figure at her side. The apparitions were quickly replaced by Sophia and Henry in battlescarred armor.

Sophia's appearance had also changed as a result of the fight. Her cybernetic forearm was almost completely skinned. She now wore a blue Ancient Oriental style blouse with a black skirt and her hair was tied back in a long braid which looked as though someone had made a rope out of pure gold.

"I take it we won," Karl commented, hoping the answer was *yes*.

"Technically," Henry replied.

"Technically?" Karl inquired.

"That's the good news," Lightening stated.

"Part of this does depend on how negotiations are handled between the captain and Lord Baldassara," the black man answered.

"Lord Baldassara?"

"He's what they call a Lord General of the Syndicate," Sophia explained, trying to avoid looking at her left arm. "He is one of most powerful men in the galaxy with an entire fleet of pirates to back him up."

"And, he answers directly to the triad."

Henry took over, receiving a glare from the alien girl.

"And known for making short work of small time pirate captains when he drafts them into his fleet."

"And who's the poor fellow with that job?" Karl asked, wondering what this really had to do with him.

"Well, we considered Reginia." Henry seemed hesitant to answer. "She was the most popular choice," he continued. "Mr. Long always wanted to be captain, but-"

"Congratulations," Lightening interrupted, climbing up Karl's shirt before perching on his shoulders. "You're now a captain. I assume you'll want someone to take the place of the parrot."

What?! How?! he thought, trying to keep calm. "You're joking right?" *They couldn't possibly...*

"Sorry," Sophia stated, fingering the hilt of the energy sword wedged between her belt and her hip.

A woman in a purple cloak with a glass axe dangling from her hip entered the room.

With her long silver hair, Karl immediately recognized her as a Lecaran. However, her hood was pulled too far down to make out the upper portion of her face.

"Lord Baldassara requests your presence," said the hooded woman. "I would advise that you come immediately. My master does not like to be kept waiting."

Sophia and the hooded woman left for Karl to get dressed.

Karl was then escorted by Henry and the cloaked woman to a room with a silver haired alien, which Karl believed to be Lord Baldassara.

A little young for a criminal mastermind, Karl thought, looking at the man in front of him seated at a desk.

The man was barely a decade older than him, nowhere near as old as the Claymore-like man that he'd been expecting to see.

I guess since I'm a captain and I am only 19- wait a minute, has it passed my birthday?

His two escorts disappeared, leaving Karl with the Syndicate leader.

"So, Terran, what is the reason for this?" Baldassara stated. The ruby eyed man stared at Karl as though he was looking into his very soul. "They called you captain, placing not one but two ships under your command. Yet you were aboard the ship for less than a month."

Karl was reluctant to say anything, as he was only placed in command for the sake of having someone for Baldassara to direct his attention towards.

The now Captain Sabers was also aware that should he displease

150

the other pirate captain, his life could end at any moment. He glanced over at the door in hopes that someone would come to his aid.

"I just -"

"So much acquired in such a little time," he stated, "would make you an excellent addition to the Syndicate."

"What?" Karl asked in disbelief.

"Congratulations," Lightening commented, scratching his ear. "You moved up from piracy to organized crime."

"I understand this is a lot to take in," said the man with metallic silver hair. "Especially after such a battle, I would understand wanting to take some time to think about the situation. However, I would advise taking us up on the offer sooner rather than later. You've managed to make enemies of the Blood Terrans and you already had the bounty hunters tailing you to begin with. We can offer you protection from both forces as one of us."

Karl was about to say something before the door behind him slid open.

"Captain," said the voice of Sophia as she entered the room. "We've loaded the Lancer."

"You!" Baldassara's eyes widened upon seeing the woman of his own race. He immediately rose from his seat and rushed over to Sophia before grabbing her hand and kissing it. Sophia quickly pulled her hand back and stepped away from the ruby eyed man. "Do you not recognize me?"

She raised her right arm showing the blue crystal slave bracelet around her wrist.

"I see," he said with disappointment upon seeing Sophia's slave bracelet. "I can't imagine what it's been like for you all these years."

"Excuse me," Karl interrupted, feeling left out of the conversation. "What exactly is your relationship to Sophia?"

"If you must know, she is my niece," Baldassara answered. "And before the fall of the empire she was also my betrothed."

"Betrothed!" Karl blurted. *Her uncle and her fiancé.* Karl quickly tried to push the thought out of his head. Sophia herself showed no reaction to the statement.

"Of course, that's all in the past," Baldassara stated, turning away from the girl. "I can't imagine what you've been through." He turned back to Karl. "I trust my niece has been treated with the utmost care while in your hands."

"Yes, sir," Sophia spoke up. "Karl has attempted to defend my life on a number of occasions."

"Attempted?" Karl whispered to the girl.

"You both owe your lives to me, remember," Lightening stated, rubbing himself against Sophia's ankles.

"You weren't much help against the Inquisitor," Sophia replied, glaring down at the feline.

Baldassara laughed slightly at the three in front of him. "I guess I'll have to thank you for that."

The hooded woman entered the room. She unveiled her face, revealing her grayish green eyes.

"What's with her?" Karl asked

"She's a halfbreed," answered Baldassara. "The offspring of a Terran and a Lecaran."

Half human! Karl thought with excitement. *That means...* Karl glanced over at Sophia. *We're genetically compatible! That means that she and I can...*

"Captain Sabers," Baldassara stated, bringing Karl back to reality. "Now in regards to my niece's placement among your crew."

"I wish to remain with my captain," Sophia spoke up. "Karl has proven himself invaluable. His ignorance, notwithstanding, will be extremely valuable in times to come. Perhaps even as a knight of the empire."

"Very well," Baldassara said, somewhat puzzled.

He turned and pointed to Karl.

"However, should his loyalty waiver, I will not hesitate to have him dealt with. Both our peoples spent many thousands of years developing wonderful methods of execution. Firing Squad. Space Suffocation. Guillotine. Banishment to the surface of Venus. The Wheel. Or I'll just crack you over the head."

"You forgot Death by Pit of Lions," Lightening contributed.

"Right, I forgot that one."

"Thanks for reminding him," said Karl to the cat.

Chapter 19- Pirates vs. Bounty Hunters

"Having any luck?" Surge glanced over at Ray as the latter appropriated the captain's chair on the small bridge.

"No," Ray replied. "All we know is they left the Dainare System after selling their cargo to agents of the abolitionist union. After that, we couldn't get any leads."

Denise stared at a small screen projecting from her console as the others discussed the major bounty. She sighed as she repeated the same motion of scrolling her finger across the list of small time bounties that might be close by to earn them some pocket change. *They'll all get hungry in a few minutes and I won't have to look at these anymore,* she thought, suddenly seeing a name and profile picture which she recognized.

Wanted alive- Karl Sabers
Offense- ship jumping
Bounty- 60,000 Titan Cronos
Last known location- Gamma province Tau Ceti IV
Status- the suspect is believed to be unarmed and is often accompanied by Lecaran slave girl and an orange tabby cat. It is recommended that this suspect be stunned.

My brother's out here in deep space and he's a criminal, she thought with disbelief, while looking at her brother's criminal profile. *How in Tartarus did this happen? He must've come looking for me. How am I going to help? Dear Father, give me strength and make sure my brother-* she began to pray, but was quickly interrupted by a beeping sound and her brother's profile began to flash red.

Wanted dead or alive- Karl Sabers
Offense- piracy, theft of sacred artifacts, theft of advanced weaponry, and ship jumping
Bounty- 80,000,000 Titan Cronos
Last known location- 70 hours ago, Reharal orbital station
Status- the suspect is in possession of a Lancer type starfighter. He is believed to have taken residence on a small Luna class star liner which has been converted to a gunship. Recent reports suggest that

their vessel was likely damaged in the recent Blood Terran attack. He is currently being accompanied by Lecaran slave registered as LG0495238.

"What!" Denise yelled out loud without realizing it. All eyes of the *Crimson Blade* turned towards her. *Shoot, I've got to hide this!* she thought quickly, tried to close her screen, but it was too late. Kira appeared behind her and saw Karl's criminal record.

"Look what Denise found," Kira stated, before tapping the link under 'LG0495238'. Ray came around and pulled up the product description for the young Lecaran girl

"Ruby red eyes, metallic gold hair, blood type L4," Ray read off of Denise's screen. "I think she's actually found a lead."

"Really?" Surge asked in surprise.

"It's not much, but it's something," Ray commented. "If they just left Reharal after it was attacked, the only close by pirate haven is going to be the Dainare System."

"That'll work," Surge agreed, raising himself up in his chair. "Seems a little predictable but that would be their only option."

"There is a small asteroid belt orbiting a brown dwarf star," B-10 stated without turning to the others. "It'll be logical they might seek refuge there."

"B-10, set an intercept course," Surge said, jumping up with a smile. "We'll be able to strike them and collect the biggest bounty any of us has ever seen."

This is awful, Denise thought, as the red ship slipped into a starless pocket of space enroute for their battle with the pirate ship.

Meanwhile, onboard the *Lady Eris*, the new pirate, Captain Karl Sabers, sat in front of a table staring at the projected image of a nearby star system hovering above the table in front of them. Standing around the table to his right were Sophia and Alice, to his left were Henry, Gavin, Zrela, Calidi, Ellris, and the former first mate, Mr. Long.

"You can't possibly be suggesting that we abandon the *Lady Eris*!" Zrela let out.

"Captain, I'll attest the ship is damaged but she's certainly not beyond simple repairs," Gavin stated, defending their ship. "And her weapon systems are far superior to that cargo ship and another thing-"

"Captain, the ship's our home." Reginia's voice came from a small holo-screen that appeared in front of Karl.

Karl looked into the florescent blue eyes of a blurred charcoal gray humanoid silhouette against the pitch black background of the virtual window in front of him. "I'm not suggesting that we abandon the ship," Karl stated, looking at each member of his crew. "I merely suggest that we keep the *Lady Eris* out of sight and switch over to the *Starlight* for the moment. Our enemies have seen this ship and will know what to look for. If we use the other ship to resupply ourselves and get this ship repaired, then leave this section of space with both the *Lady Eris* and the *Star-*"

"Actually, Captain," Henry spoke up. "We've decided to rename the new ship. After the unanimous vote of the crew, the new starship shall be named *Draco*."

"I've heard that name before," Lightening said, jumping onto Karl's shoulder.

You didn't want to use the ship, but you've already renamed her, Karl thought, looking at the small brown sphere surrounded by a ring of debris. *Now if we can just get the ship ready to go. Then, with the Devil's Fang, that will make three ships in my fleet.*

They all began to turn away from the star chart projection as a small red dot appeared adjacent to the green one representing their vessel.

"Is this thing real time?" asked Karl.

"Yes," Gavin answered. "Why do you ask?"

"MEOW!" Lightening abruptly yelped, drowning out Karl's next word.

Karl slapped his forehead as the red dot drew even closer to the *Lady Eris*. "Battle stations and brace for impact!" The ship jolted.

"What did they hit?!" Karl yelled.

"We have light damage to the dorsal engine," Zrela replied.

Another red dot appeared approaching their starboard bow.

"Return fire!" Karl commanded.

"We can't!" Gavin informed. "Weapon systems are offline and our turrets are locked on each other."

"What!" Karl yelled, squeezing the armrest of his captain's chair. *This can't be happening!* "Avoid it if we can't shoot it down." *Why aren't our systems working?* Karl looked around the bridge, hoping to figure out some way to overcome the situation. Within seconds, the blast doors slammed down over the corridors leading out of the bridge.

"This is Surge, captain of the *Crimson Blade*," said a voice from the ship's intercom. "Surrender your vessel and hand over the pirate known as Karl Sabers, and his slave girl, or we will destroy your ship."

The eyes of the crew were trained upon Karl and Sophia.

Karl reached for his sword and turned his gaze to Sophia.

"Well, Captain," Long stated with an almost pleased tone in his voice. "Sorry, it had to end this way."

The blonde man turned towards the others.

"Restrain them."

The crew did nothing.

"You heard the message, give them to the bounty hunter."

"If the bounty hunter really can take out this ship with no effort, why then would he let any of us go? Why would he only want the captain and his girl?" Henry questioned.

"He's right," Zrela agreed. "We all have a price on our heads."

Calidi and Ellris extended their Halberds and pointed them at the former first mate.

"Baldassara has an interest in these two," Ellris stated. "If you betray them, you'll be making all of us enemies of the Syndicate."

As the rest of the crew stared intently at Mr. Long, the doors leading into the bridge popped open and a golden disk surrounded by four transparent crystals orbiting around its edges wandered onto the bridge. Except for Henry, Karl, and Sophia, all the crew members turned their weapons towards the Oracle in panic. The crystals immediately turned yellow and backed away.

"What the hell is this thing?" yelled Gavin.

"An enemy drone?" Zrela questioned

"I am the- " the Oracle paused for a moment, "the magnificent Oracle of the Elders and-"

"Just who I needed," Karl stated. "Can you do anything about the guns?"

The Oracle tilted itself towards Karl.

"Captain!"

Karl then realized that the rest of the crew was still aiming at the floating disc.

"He's with us."

The pirates slowly lowered their weapons.

"Can you fix the lock down on ship's guns?" Karl persisted.

The crystal around the Oracle turned orange.

"Hold on."

The *Lady Eris'* gun torrents locked onto the *Crimson Blade* and beams of green and blue streaked towards the small red ship. The bounty hunter ship quickly sped off, trying to evade the shots from the pirate ship.

"I thought their weapon systems were down!" Surge yelled, as the ship jolted.

"They were," Ray replied. "Someone's overridden the hack."

"Return fire!" Surge commanded.

The wings of the smaller ship folded open at a 90 degree angle at the stern of the vessel as a volley of missiles launched from the keel. The *Crimson Blade,* streaked toward the *Lady Eris.* As the missiles were shot down by the pirate ship, the *Crimson Blade* flipped over displaying her bow directly at the *Lady Eris.*

"Prepare the Particle Blade," Surge commanded.

"Particle what?" Denise asked.

"Roger," B-10 replied. A red joystick with a glass trigger rose in front of Surge's seat.

"Surge, don't do it!" Ray yelled.

"Fire another round of missiles and target her keel beam turrets," Surge said with a smirk, ignoring Ray's warning. "You're about to see why the ship is named the *Crimson Blade*." He squeezed the trigger plunging the vessel of the bounty hunters into darkness.

A thick red beam of glowing particles shot from the bow of the *Crimson Blade* striking one of the gun turrets of the *Lady Eris.* However, instead of disappearing, the red beam of particles then panned along the topside of the *Lady Eris,* completely obliterating her dorsal turrets and cutting away her only functional engine.

The red particle blade vanished, leaving the volley of missiles to strike the underside of the pirate ship.

Chapter 20- A Brief Reunion

After a few moments, he realized Mr. Long was no longer among the crew still trapped on the broken vessel.

"Damage report!" Karl demanded turning to Gavin.

"It'll be easier just to tell you what still works," he answered. "We still have life support, portside engine is still attached. With minor repairs we should be able to jump to the nearest planet. The dorsal engine is still floating around out there, but we might reattach it and use it again as well. One of the keel turrets is still mostly intact, but it will take some time to restore power to it."

"Alice, Gavin, head down to engineering," Karl commanded. "See if you can't get the ship back online and get us out of here."

"If it's any consolation," said the Oracle. "The enemy ship also appears to be inactive."

"Captain," said the voice of Reginia through Karl's handheld. "I regret to inform you that a small shuttle appears to have been deployed from the enemy vessel. I think they intend to board us."

"Is there anything we can do to stop them?" asked Karl.

"We are detecting four intruders," Zrela stated.

"There's a chance we might be able to intercept them," Henry suggested, "however, three appear to be leaving the shuttle and splitting up."

"Alice, Gavin, take the Oracle and try to get our systems back online," Karl commanded. "Everyone else break into groups of two and deal with the intruders on our way to their shuttle. Sophia is with me, Calidi with Ellris, and I guess Reginia with Henry."

"Captain," Sophia spoke up. "Perhaps it would be best if you went with Henry and I'll go after the shuttle."

Karl turned to Sophia. "Are you sure about this?"

"I'll meet up with Reginia," she answered.

"Ellris and I can handle each bounty hunter individually," Calidi added.

"Okay," Karl stated. He departed with Lightening and Henry.

As the three made their way from the bridge down the corridor towards the hanger, a copper haired Lecaran appeared before them with a katana at his side.

Karl pulled his sword as Surge gripped his hand around the

dragon hilt of his katana.

The bronze mouth of the dragon opened and six pencil sized rockets fired from the hilt.

Karl activated his light buckler.

The mini-warheads smashed against the round disc of plasma in an explosion of orange and red.

The bounty hunter came at the pirate, drawing his sword in a flash.

The orange blade blocked the now activated blue charge-cutter field of the katana.

Karl staggered back as another swing came from the blue blade.

Karl blocked the attack with his buckler and Surge's weapon bounced off his force field. Karl slashed at his enemy and Surge jumped back before swinging his sword in a wide arch.

Karl ducked below the Asian sword and caught the blade with the hook of his sickle sword.

Karl jerked the sword of his enemy away and the plasma derringer extended from under his left sleeve.

The pirate pointed the pistol directly at Surge's throat.

"Should I finish things off right here?" Karl asked, his finger on the trigger. Surge dropped his katana and raised his hands in the air. "Now maybe I can get some answers. Why is everyone so interested in Sophia?"

"Why would a bounty hunter need a reason to go after a pirate?"

"Not a good answer." Karl jabbed the barrel into Surge's throat.

"Karl is not very good at recognizing the obvious," Lightening stated. "You will have to try again."

"Some Lecaran calling himself Dergan Fafnir put a bounty on her head for 1,000,000,000," Surge answered. "As for you, you're just more pirate scum that needs to be eradicated from the galaxy."

Upon hearing that comment, Karl hit Surge across the head with the knuckle guard of his sword.

Karl then turned to Henry.

"Tie him up in the cargohold. We'll figure out what to do with him after we deal with his companions."

Unknown to Surge, B-10, and Kira, Denise remained hidden in the arms locker until they were gone.

She made her way out of the shuttle and into the main hanger with her hook swords.

Her hope was that she would be able to avoid any other crew members before finding her brother.

She was wrong.

Denise looked upon the woman with long golden hair.

Her skinned mechanical hand now resembled a black metal claw.

Denise looked into the woman's ruby red eyes as the plasma coil around her wrist uncoiled and extended into a yellow plasma blade.

"The Ruby Eyed Empress!" Denise let out in shock.

Denise ignited the beam cutters on each of her hook swords and charged at the woman who blocked the two beams with her plasma sword before drawing a glass knife with her right hand.

Sophia slashed at Denise with her dagger.

Denise jumped back barely dodging the dagger's swing.

"What did you say?" Sophia asked, as her dagger turned blue. "Are you from other lost colonies as well?"

"I don't know what you did to make my brother join you," Denise stated, "but I'll make sure you pay for this!"

Denise came at Sophia again with the sword in her right hand striking Sophia's wrist blade before coming at Sophia's right side with the sword in her left hand.

Sophia attempted to block the second sword with her dagger.

However, her blade missed the purple beam and instead struck a solid piece of Denise's sword, splitting it in half and the beam vanished in an instant.

Sophia kneed Denise in the stomach.

Denise released her hold on the weapon in her left hand and staggered back.

"So, you're Karl's sister," Sophia stated, as she approached Denise. "If you're willing to surrender-"

Sophia stopped the second she heard footsteps racing towards her left side. She then turned to see Kira charging at her. Sophia swung her sword at the furry eared alien girl.

Kira jumped up, dodging the swing of the energy blade. She kicked Sophia in the chest, knocking her to the ground.

After confirming that Sophia was unconscious, the catgirl turned to Denise.

"Are you okay, Denise?" Kira asked. "Isn't that the girl we were supposed to capture?"

"I think you're right," Denise commented, remembering the bounty description.

She broke one of my swords, though, Denise thought, looking at her damaged weapon.

"Wait till the others hear about this," commented Kira as she pulled out her handheld. "Surge! We've got her."

There was no reply.

"Surge. Surge, Surge! Are you there?!"

Denise walked over to Kira's handheld. "Surge! Answer us!"

"This is Captain Karl Sabers," said the voice of Denise's brother. "To the bounty hunters who have boarded my ship, we've captured your leader and demand your immediate surrender."

"Karl?!" Denise was in shock.

She could not believe what she was hearing.

Her brother was not only a pirate but was their captain!

"Denise?!" said Karl's voice over the handheld. "Denise, is that you? What are you doing there?"

Kira muted her handheld and turned to Denise. "You know this criminal?"

"He's my- " she hesitated.

"Kira! Denise!" came Ray's voice over Kira's handheld. "I've checked the buildup in the center hold of the pirate ship. You guys need to get out of there! That ship's about to explode!"

"Wh-"

Before Denise even had a chance to say anything, Kira grabbed both Sophia and Denise as a shock wave rippled through the ship.

The center hull of the *Lady Eris* opened up into a ball of orange and white flames which disappeared in an instant.

The ship buckled in as the stern and bow forced away from each other with shards of metal flying in every direction like shrapnel, which rained upon the *Crimson Blade*.

"Denise, wake up!" Kira cried, shaking Denise.

"Kira, stop!" Denise demanded, her ears still ringing from the explosion. "I'm already awake!"

Having remained fully coherent, she had merely shut her eyes in reaction to the detonation.

She began rubbing her head, before seeing the detached bow section of the *Lady Eris* drifting outside.

"That's where Surge and Karl are!"

"Who's Karl?"

"My-" Denise was suddenly interrupted by the humming sound coming from the other side of the bulkhead.

"Denise, Kira!" Ray called over Kira's handheld. "Can you guys hear me?!"

"Yes," Kira answered. "We've got the target, but Surge is on the other section the ship."

"Great," Ray stated, as a glowing orange circle appeared on the side of the hull. "How did that manage to happen? Never mind. I'll be over there to pick you up in a moment. Then we'll grab him."

A round slab of metal fell down and dropped to the floor, revealing a boarding tube leading to the *Crimson Blade*.

Kira and Denise picked up the still unconscious Sophia.

Kira taking her torso and the human taking her legs.

As they made their way towards the entrance of the *Crimson Blade,* Sophia's right ankle slipped out of Denise's hand knocking off her glass shoe.

Now that the *Lady Eris* had been blown in half, the *Crimson Blade* detached herself from the *Lady Eris*.

The red ship then departed for the bow section of the pirate ship to retrieve Surge.

Karl opened his eyes to see a floating cat.

His arm was throbbing at the pain from slamming into the bulkhead.

What did the bounty hunters do to my ship? Karl thought, looking at the body of Surge also still drifting unconsciously. *Did they intend to sacrifice one of their own?*

"Lightening!"

"I thought you guys had this zero gravity thing fixed," the feline commented, wildly swinging his paws in the air. "Do something!"

"I think we have more to worry about than the discomforts of zero gravity," Karl commented, before pulling out his handheld. "Gavin, stasis report!"

There was no reply.

"Henry, are you there?" Karl asked.

"I'm here," Henry replied. "But I'm trapped on the other side of this bulkhead. What happened?"

"Your guess is as good as mine," Karl answered. "Have you been able to get in contact with anyone else?"

"No," he answered, as Surge began to move. "I'll see if I can't access another part of the ship from the outside."

"What happened?" asked the bounty hunter.

"So you're the one who bought my sister," Karl Sabers' glowing orange blade appeared.

"Your sister?" Surge said in shock. "Denise is the sister of a pirate who would blow up his own ship?"

"What do you mean?" asked Karl. "Your allies must've have set off the explosion."

"You think I was dumb enough to destroy a ship that I was on!" Surge reacted, taking offense to Karl's statement.

If the bounty hunters didn't set off the explosion, that means there is a traitor among us! Karl thought, his eyes still fixated on Surge.

Without warning, the bulkhead door behind him slid open, revealing the Oracle and another man with blonde hair.

"You see, Mr. Long," said the Oracle. "I told you I would find them."

"Yes, you've proven quite useful," said Mr. Long, as he floated towards the bounty hunter.

"What are you doing?" asked Karl.

"It shouldn't really matter to you now," he answered, pulling a pistol on Karl. "Bounty hunter, when is your ship coming along to get you?"

"What are you talking about?" asked Surge.

"I'll be hitching a ride with you," Mr. Long answered. "All you have to do is take me over to Fafnir."

163

"So you're the one who set off the explosion," Karl stated, as he slowly floated towards the back wall.

"That's right," said Mr. Long. "I was hoping that the detonation would finish you off while I remained in an escape pod. Unfortunately, I'll have to let the bounty hunter take you alive."

As soon as Mr. Long turned his gaze towards Surge, Karl pushed against the wall and launched himself at the blonde Terran.

With an upward slice from the activated Orange blade, Karl sliced off Mr. Long's right arm mid-trigger pull.

"Surge!" said the voice of Ray, over his handheld. "We're ready for pickup."

A red blast from Mr. Long's pistol tore open a hole in the bulkhead door opening up to the vacuum of space.

Surge exhaled and shut his eyes as he was sucked out into space. Within a matter of seconds, he was grabbed by B-10 who immediately pulled him into the *Crimson Blade*.

The one armed Mr. Long was sucked out into space, and Karl was soon to follow when a glowing beam of light grabbed onto both him and Lightening.

Karl looked up at the Oracle pulling him and the cat towards it.

A liquid substance sprayed at the open bulkhead, forming a film that resealed the section.

With the bounty hunters' departure, the separated pirate crew was able to use a small shuttlecraft to ferry the trapped individuals to the stern section, which still had artificial gravity and full life support capability.

The majority of the surviving crew congregated in the ship's main hanger. Only the rock group, the Clearances, was isolated in the brig since their incessant playing was driving some of the crew insane.

Karl would have to deal with them later.

"So Mr. Long was working with the bounty hunters," Henry commented, as he glanced over at Karl, who was sitting down on a toolbox rubbing his forehead.

"It's not possible to tell how long this was going on, but chances are it happened after we made Karl Sabers captain," Gavin speculated.

"I never would've thought that he would've betrayed us, though," said Zrela.

"I don't know. The bounty hunter found us awfully fast after we left Karl with the Evlon cult," Alice added.

"But they were actually targeting Sophia at that point," Zrela replied. "We were battling the fanatics at that time."

Sophia is gone, Karl thought, looking down at Sophia's glass shoe in his left hand.

And Denise is with the man who took her.

The yellow-orange feline walked over to Karl and began rubbing himself against his legs.

"Captain," said the voice of Reginia through Karl's handheld. "I regret to inform you that both Calidi and Ellris are neither onboard the ship nor within the debris field, and the small vessel the bounty hunters came on is gone. The Lancer fighter, however, is still in operational order."

Calidi and Ellris are gone too. Were they working with the bounty hunters as well? Karl thought.

The situation seemed to get worse and worse.

One fighter's not going to do much good trying to get Sophia back.

"Are you going to follow the same strategy that you did while chasing down your sister?" asked Lightening.

165

"Captain," Alice stated, coming towards him with one of the handhelds from the *Nomad*. "We found this in one of the cells where we kept your companions from the *Starlight*."

She handed the device over to Karl.

"Good morning, I am Hologram 718209, for your convenience I have been programmed to respond to the name Miss Holo," the AI greeted them as her face appeared on the screen

"Where did you come from?" asked Karl. "I thought the council rewrote your program."

"Hello, Mr. Sabers," she stated. "I made a backup of myself before I was downloaded into the Koal ship's computer system."

Denise sat guarding Sophia, who was now imprisoned in a small closet which had been converted into a cell.

Ray had taken the alien girl's damaged left arm and she looked completely unbalanced with only one shoe and one arm.

"Now that we have you," Denise said.

The alien girl sat up.

"What is your relationship to my brother?"

"My relationship," Sophia smiled slightly. "That depends entirely on the situation at hand."

Denise just stood and glared at the alien woman.

"First he was my owner and master, then he was my ally, and finally my captain. For the moment, you can call him my left hand man if you want something to cover the entire period of time. At this point, you should be more concerned with your relationship with him."

I can't believe this. My brother, a slave owner? A pirate? This woman's ally?

"How did this happen?"

"You'll have to ask him," Sophia replied. "I'm more interested in whether or not you actually know why you were sent after me."

"It won't matter in a few moments," Surge commented as he walked into the room. "We're about to rendezvous at the Neith base."

The battlescarred *Crimson Blade* exited dark space just outside of a hollowed out asteroid, which had been converted into a starbase. She drew closer to the familiar gold and black frigate as she passed through the base's atmospheric shield. A boarding tube extended

166

towards the bounty hunter's vessel.

Sophia was pulled from the closet by her one arm with a tug from Kira. Waiting at the end of the boarding tube was an old Lecaran with a thick black beard.

The Lecaran escorted the bounty hunters and their prisoner down a catwalk towards a large iron door which separated the hanger from a hallway.

Their escort opened the door leading to an office with two occupants. The first was a silver haired yellow eyed Lecaran dressed in a white coat trimmed in gold. The second was his armored associate with a triple lens eyepiece on the left side of his helmet.

"So, you have brought us a suspect," said Fafnir. "Well, I believe the first half of the payment is in order."

Surge lifted up his handheld as half the bounty was transferred over to them.

"You will be contacted once her identification is concluded."

"Captain, are you sure about this?" asked Gavin, looking down at the Lancer.

"Don't worry about it," Karl answered with a confident smirk. The patch began to close over the cockpit. "Just make sure the *Lady Eris* and the *Draco* are ready when I give the signal." With the hatch seal blocking all outside sound, Karl let out a deep sigh.

"Liar," Lightening stated.

Karl threw the cat a glare, before turning his attention to the floating disk an inch above his dashboard. "Are you sure this will work, Oracle?"

"Yes, sir," the Oracle replied. "With the *Lady Eris*' dorsal engine we should just be able to make it to that military outpost."

"Then they will mistake this engine pod for an oncoming starship," Karl stated, repeating the plan. "And then we abandon it as our decoy. Got it."

Karl made the sign of the cross.

The fighter and the engine pod were engulfed in a bright light and vanished from that section of space.

The cylindrical engine and fighter appeared just outside of an asteroid field. The Lancer detached from the cylindrical engine. The fighter raced towards the asteroid, concealing the starport.

167

A squadron of diamond shaped starfighters with forward-swept wings were deployed to intercept the engine pod. Karl's fighter slipped by undetected.

As he approached, he saw the *Crimson Blade* docked beside a black and gold frigate.

Now that's an impressive looking ship, Karl thought, fantasizing about having that vessel as his new flagship.

"So, Princess," said Fafnir, as he stared at Sophia through the force field covering her cell. "You thought you could get away with hiding out among pirates. How did you manage to escape the execution?"

"I have no idea what you're talking about," Sophia stated. "If I was an heir to the royal family, why would anyone have allowed me to be sold off as an ordinary slave?"

"Of course, your protectors saw fit to wipe your memory, thinking that would prevent us from locating you," Fafnir commented.

He drew a metal capped glass cylinder filled with a green liquid from his coat. He placed it against Sophia's neck. Her eyes became heavy as she fell into a trance-like state.

"Now, why don't you tell us who you really are?"

"I am Princess Vearas," she answered.

Fafnir's look of satisfaction quickly turned to one of shock and dread.

"Fourth daughter of the Sargoth of the Neith Empire and second in line to the throne."

"You can't be," Fafnir stated in disbelief. "You're Vlora, the Princess who escaped the execution and is first in line to the throne. None of the others survived."

Sophia suddenly snapped out of her trance before looking him directly in the eye with her ruby red irises. "I was at the execution," she stated. "I remember standing there with my mother, father, and all of my siblings except the oldest, as the yellow bolts of plasma rained down upon us burning away my left arm."

She grinned at him. "How does it feel? Knowing that you got the wrong sister? That all of your work has been for nothing and that my sister is still out there just waiting to take the throne and cast down the government you serve?"

"Tell me where she is!" Fafnir demanded.

"I don't know," she answered. "However, considering what you went through to find me and that you thought I was her, I doubt you will find her."

"We'll see about that," he answered. "You might not be the right princess, but you could function as bait. Once you and your sister are dead, the monarchists will have no one to rally around and the Federation will be spared from the madness of-" The door slid open behind him before he had a chance to finish his statement.

"Sir," said the voice of a Lecaran man with his face half hidden by a helmet. "I regret to inform you that there are intruders who have infiltrated our security."

"Deal with them at once," Fafnir said, not even looking at the young man's face. "I can't afford to have any interruptions."

The man drew an axe from his side, which within a few seconds extended into a halberd.

"I'm afraid I cannot allow you to lay another hand on Her Highness." At that statement his blade turned yellow and he charged at Fafnir.

Fafnir watched the yellow blade come towards him, only for it to strike a blue glass halberd in the hand of the armored soldier at his side. "So, a former member of the royal guard. Take care of him." Fafnir pulled a handheld from his pocket. "Sound the alarms!"

"Now students," said the voice of Miss Holo as she appeared upon Fafnir's handheld. "Can you tell me what creature mysteriously disappeared 40 years a-?"

Fafnir threw down his handheld in rage.

"Karl," said the Oracle. "They seem to have found us."

"Great," Karl said, gripping the Lancer's weapon controls. "I thought you and Miss Holo were supposed to prevent that."

"This is what happens when you rely on robots," Lightening added.

"I prefer the term artificial life form," the Oracle replied. "And we're not the only ones here. It appears that Calidi was able to infiltrate this base as well and it would be reasonable to assume that Ellris is with him."

"We'll have to see about those two later," Karl stated, as two fighters appeared in front of them. "Oracle, launch the engine pod at the station now."

As the two enemy fighters came at the Lancer, Karl fired a single shot from the main gun and shattered the first of the two fighters into several fragments.

Then he opened fire with the two guns mounted within the forward facing claws of his fighter.

The Neith fighter returned fire striking the left engine of the Lancer.

The resulting explosion from the engine made the Lancer crash into the wall of the base.

The Lancer's cockpit ejected from the rest of the fighter.

Karl's craft and the diamond shaped fighter destroyed each other in a blaze of blue and red.

The ejected cockpit hovered next to a catwalk for a few seconds.

With his pistol in hand and his sickle sword at his side, Karl and Lightening immediately jumped out.

The Oracle floated behind them.

Karl looked back for a second to see the Lancer's cockpit drift away before being destroyed by enemy fire.

Karl quickly turned toward the Oracle. "Which way is she?"

"Turn right," the Oracle replied.

The three made their way down the catwalk.

Two guards appeared before them and opened fire.

Karl raised his light buckler and a round force field blanketed the three of them from the enemy shots.

Two soldiers drew their swords and charged at the Terran.

One of them was tripped by Lightening.

Distracted by his stumbling companion, the other was gunned down by a green beam from Karl's energy pistol.

Another set of guards appeared from behind only to be cut down by the slash of a red halberd.

Ellris stood before him with his halberd pointed at Karl.

"So you're the ones who blew my cover," Karl stated, pointing his weapon at the alien in front of him. "What are you even doing?"

"I suppose at this point it wouldn't make any difference," Calidi said with a displeased expression. "Ellris and I were part of her highness's royal bodyguards, and as our final orders before our nation fell to the rebellion, we were charged with protecting the last heir to

170

the empire and ensuring their return to the throne. Now, what reason do you have to be here? You are neither from the kingdom of Neith or even a member of our race."

"He's trying to save his love interest," Lightening stated.

"Not a-" Karl was about to say something in response to the cat's statement but stopped before the words could make it out of his mouth.

Lightening might have a point.

While he could not say at this point that he loved Sophia, he certainly couldn't imagine life without her.

"Regardless of my reason, our goals are the same. Are you going to work with me to save her, or not?"

Calidi lowered his weapon. "Very well, Terran."

"I believe you're supposed to address him as 'Captain'," Lightening stated, wiping his face with his paw.

The two men, the cat, and the Oracle raced towards Fafnir along the catwalk leading to a hallway lined with metal doors.

A green bladed glass halberd came at Karl from a bearded Lecaran.

Karl blocked the green weapon with his light buckler before drawing his own weapon.

"I'll handle this traitor," Calidi stated, recognizing the man in front as a former member of the Royal Guard. "Keep in mind, Captain, if you fail you will be dealt with."

"My side won the war," said their enemy, as Calidi raised his weapon. "With the monarchy gone, that makes you the traitor."

Calidi charged at the man while Karl, Lightening, and the Oracle made their way to the attacker.

There he saw a silver haired Lecaran man making his way out of one room dragging the one armed woman by a bronze shackle.

Karl activated the charge-cutter field in his sickle sword as he stood before Fafnir.

Fafnir attached the other end of the chain to the wall before drawing a glass single edged short sword from his side.

The sword turned a lightish red.

"So you're the Terran who's caused all this trouble. You, among others, should want her dead." Fafnir came at Karl, who blocked the swing with his orange blade. "Her family is responsible for taking the

Earth from your people and banishing your kind into space."

"It doesn't matter what her ancestors did to mine," Karl stated, kicking Fafnir back. "The ones who stole Earth and the ones who lost it are long dead. Sophia is my comrade in the here and now."

Karl slashed at the alien striking the reddish sword.

Fafnir twisted the sickle sword away from Karl and came at the Terran with a dagger in his left hand.

Within seconds, Karl activated his light buckler which met the oncoming dagger head on.

Karl kicked the dagger out of Fafnir's hand.

Fafnir's glass sword slid against Karl's blade striking, the knuckle guard of the weapon.

Karl shifted his body to the right and Fafnir's sword slipped back to the beginning of the curve on Karl's khopesh.

Karl released his grip on his sword's ring-like trigger and the weapon turned back into transparent glass as the glowing straight sword severed the sickle from the unsharpened ricasso, leaving only a stray piece of glass with a diagonal cut attached to the hand guard.

With the curved section of glass still flying in the air, Karl twisted his hand and ran the four inch glass shard through Fafnir's chest.

The alien man staggered back and fell on the floor yellow blood dripping from Karl's broken sword.

"You came for me," Sophia stated. "And you know who I am now?"

"I don't see where that changes anything. Other than maybe what I'm supposed to call you now."

Karl picked up Fafnir's glass sword and slashed the chain holding Sophia's right arm.

Sophia dropped into Karl's arms.

She opened her ruby red eyes and looked up at the pirate.

Karl reached behind his back and pulled the glass shoe from his belt.

"I thought you might be missing this."

"Cinderella," Lightening commented. "You came all this way to bring her back a shoe. I know you two are about to give into your hormones, but it's probably best to do this another time after we escape!"

Sophia stood up and slipped her shoe back on. "Which way is

your ship?"

They quickly made their way into a control room overlooking the port.

Karl paused for a moment. "Well-"

"The Lancer got blown up," Lightening commented.

"We could steal another ship," Karl stated, glancing over at the black and gold frigate. "I wish we could take that one."

"Why not," she stated. "We're probably already the most wanted people in the galaxy, and that warship's the property of the Neith Empire anyway."

"Now the question is how do you get over there and not get killed," Lightening stated, turning to the Oracle. "I guess you'll need to make yourself useful or we'll turn you into scrap metal."

"All right, all right!" said the Oracle.

The golden disk floated over to a panel underneath the window overlooking the port.

"Now let's see." The lights then flickered off. "No, that's not right."

The lights came back on and a brass gangplank extended towards the frigate, covered in a red cylindrical force field.

"We have to hurry, it won't last long."

Lightening rushed towards the side hatch on the other end of the boarding ramp.

The cat was quickly followed by the alien girl and the human pirate.

The floating disc followed close behind.

The airlock of the ship slammed shut.

On either side of them were Neith soldiers with their weapons pointed at them.

Lightening and Karl immediately looked at the Oracle.

"Guys, it'll take a moment-" Lights flashed out before the Oracle finished his statement. "That wasn't me."

The lights flickered back on slowly and they turned to see Sophia standing there with her right hand placed in a panel in the wall.

"In the presence of a royal family member," said a voice of the ship's computer coming over the intercom. "Command of this vessel now falls to her Royal Highness, Princess Vearas."

The soldiers stood dumbfounded.

"By the command of Princess Vearas," Sophia commanded, "triple gravity across the ship a meter beyond this point."

The soldiers in front of them were immediately pulled to the ground.

"Now what?" Karl asked

"Oracle," Lightening stated, looking at the floating desk.

"I should be able to dampen the gravity around us allowing us to make it to the bridge of this warship," the Oracle answered.

The all went into the dark and empty bridge of the frigate.

Sophia placed her hand on the armrest of the captain's chair.

"I believe this is your seat." She smile at him.

"I know the two of you want to establish your relationship, but I think we should focus on escaping this place first," Lightening stated.

The ship's consoles lining the walls of the bridge lit up with a multitude of colors as the ship came to life.

Karl heard a peep from his handheld.

"Calidi and Ellris have acquired a shuttle," said Miss Holo, appearing above the device. "They will be docking momentarily."

Sophia ran over to the pilot seat and Karl sat down in his chair.

The walls around them faded away into a panoramic view of the starport.

The gold and black frigate broke free from the metal moorings that were holding the ship in place and began sliding out of the port.

For a moment, it seemed as though they would escape unnoticed, but that thought left them when they saw a small red ship appear before the bow of the frigate.

"Not this again," Karl stated, looking upon the red ship.

"Oracle, you need to fix this again," said the cat.

"The ship has a Dark Space Corridor drive, not a flash drive," said the Oracle. "This won't work."

Karl noticed the floating dorsal engine from the *Lady Eris* was still mostly intact. "Can we use that?"

The dorsal engine activated and sped towards the frigate under the control of Miss Holo.

Then the engine lightly tapped the Lecaran ship and engulfed both vessels in a bright flash of yellow and orange.

The frigate reemerged into the empty void of ordinary space surrounded by stars.

As she meandered along, the completely burnt out engine from the *Lady Eris* drifted away.

"What will you do now?" asked the Oracle, still floating around the bridge.

"Don't know." Karl got to his feet. "My original goal was to get my sister back."

If it weren't for the fact that my sister had been cast out into space, I never would have left the alien ship with my fellow students. I was having a good time at the costume party, before the attack on the Nomad.

"Perhaps I should return to my fellow students who were taken from the *Nomad* and tell them of the worlds that exist beyond their stars?" he speculated aloud.

Sophia looked displeased with his comment.

"Your place is here," she said, putting her hand on the back of the captain's chair.

"Are you sure?" Karl asked, walking over to the princess. "I would expect the princess to want the closest thing there was to a throne."

"I have no intention of taking the throne for myself," she answered. "If we can find my sister, she'll be the one to take the throne."

We?

Karl mentally reacted to Sophia's statement.

The door behind them slid open and the young Ellris entered the bridge.

"I apologize for the interruption, Your Highness," he said, placing his left arm across his chest and bowing. "But what would you like done with the bounty hunter vessel?"

Sophia turned back to Karl. "I'm afraid I'm going to need to borrow that chair for a moment," said the princess, pulling the captain out of his chair, before seating herself on it.

"I just got that chair, too," Karl said under his breath.

"That goes with the territory," said the cat. "What's yours is hers,

175

what's hers is hers, and you're both mine."

Denise awoke to find the crew unconscious. The asteroid base was gone, replaced by only empty space and scattered bits of metal. She glanced to the right of the debris field and took notice of the alien warship as the double barreled turret of the frigate took aim at the *Crimson Blade*.

"Surge, wake up!" Denise yelled.

"What?" Surge asked in a daze. "What happened to the base?"

"We appear to have been shifted about a light year away from our previous position," B-10 answered. A beep from the helm awoke Ray from his slumber.

"This is Captain Karl Sabers of the starship-" said a voice over the ship's communications system.

"Still working on a name," said another voice.

"Lightening, keep quiet," Karl said, before continuing. "Her Highness, Princess Vearas Sargoth wishes to negotiate with-"

"Princess?!" Denise thought out loud in shock, interrupting her brother.

My brother, the space pirate, and the princess! She must be a fake.

"I don't negotiate with pirates," Surge replied, without a second thought.

"Surge!" stated an alarmed Ray. "They're charging weapons."

"You two stop it!" Denise yelled, glaring at Surge. "This is my brother, let's see what he has to say." She then turned towards the intercom. "What is it, Karl?"

"There is no reason to shout," Karl stated

"If you're interested," Sophia added, "I have a deal in mind that would benefit both our parties. Meanwhile, I want my arm back."

A few moments later, the *Crimson Blade* docked with the frigate consuming eighty percent of the space within the small hanger.

Surge and Denise exited their ship with the cybernetic left arm in Denise's right hand. They were greeted by Ellris and Calidi, who then escorted the two bounty hunters through the ship towards the bridge.

They arrived to find Karl standing beside the one-armed Sophia, who was seated in the captain's chair with her legs crossed.

Calidi took the cybernetic arm from Denise and handed it to the

176

princess.

Upon reattaching her left arm, the alien girl made a fist with her mechanical hand.

"Now we can begin," Sophia stated. "I would like to enlist your services in recovering Her Highness, the Crown Princess Vlora."

"Like I said, I don't negotiate with pirates," Surge replied, glaring at Karl and Sophia.

"I understand your distaste for pirates," the ruby eyed girl stated, glancing over at Karl. "Which is why I have taken the liberty of issuing Karl Sabers a letter of marque, in the name of the Neith Empire."

"In other words, legal piracy," Lightening commented.

"What?!" Denise let out.

"I am also prepared to offer you ten times the amount that Fafnir had on our heads," Sophia stated, with a smirk.

"I'm not just some random mercenary-"

"We'll take it!" Denise interrupted before Surge could finish his answer.

"Denise!" Surge exclaimed.

"Karl is my brother," Denise replied. "We can't just abandon them."

"Good to have you onboard," Karl stated.

"They're criminals. We have to arrest them," Surge argued.

Ellris and Calidi both activated their halberds in reaction to the bounty hunter's statement.

"I have to throw my vote in with Denise here," said the voice of Ray from within the bounty hunter's pocket. "With Fafnir out of the picture, collecting on the girl is next to impossible, because the Neith government is likely to deny all existence of her. And we won't be breaking any Terran laws so long as no action was taken against either Titan or Mars. The only one here with the bounty on their head is Karl Sabers at 80,000,000 Titan Cronos."

"I knew I forgot something," said the Oracle, as the crystals around him began spinning counterclockwise. "You might want to check that again."

Surge pulled out his handheld which projected a screen displaying the criminal record of Karl Sabers.

The screen suddenly vanished in a field of static and reappeared a few seconds later with a red square that read- "Statute of Limitations-Expired."

Surge stood dumbfounded for a few moments before switching the screen back over to Ray.

"So this has been a total bust," the bounty hunter sighed. "What are Kira and B-10's feelings about this?"

"As a cybernetic lifeform, I am not sure feelings is the correct term to use," B-10 stated over the handheld device in her usual monotone. "I was, however, originally designed as the navigation unit of a star cruiser, so this mission would be agreeable with my programming."

"My people are mercenaries," said Kira, coming down the corridor behind them. "Sorry, Surge, I'm with the others."

"So, I'm outvoted." Surge reluctantly walked over to Sophia, who extended her hand for him to kiss. "We won't be acting against the Mars Imperium or the Titan Empire, and will have no part in the raiding of legitimate civilian vessels."

"Agreed." Sophia offered her right-hand to be kissed.

The bounty hunter shook the princess's hand vigorously .

A grin appeared on his face. Surge was reluctant to admit it but the idea of questing after a lost princess did seem romantic to him.

Sophia pulled her hand away, a displeased expression on her face.

"I assure you that I have no intention of making an enemy of either empire," Sophia answered, looking over at Karl. "The actions of Mars or Titan, notwithstanding, we have a deal. Depending on how things work out I might even be open to setting up a place for your people on the blue planet where I was born."

"Wait!" Lightening stated, jumping onto the back of the captain's chair. "So the alien girl was born on Earth and the two humans were born in deep space, then that makes Sophia the Earthling, and Karl and Denise the aliens."

Both Karl and Denise looked blank.

"Greetings, students," said the voice of Miss Holo. "I'm sorry to disturb you, but your rather unfortunate classmates have managed to get themselves into a rather unfortunate situation on board the shuttlecraft. I would appreciate it if someone would volunteer to be of assistance."

"Okay. How the hell did they get there?" Karl asked, rolling his eyes.

"They, who?" asked Denise.

"It would appear that they jumped from the Evlon vessel during the Blood Terran attack," the hologram answered. "And it seems they have been stowed away onboard ever since."

Karl, Sophia, and Lightening made their way towards the hanger with Denise following close behind.

"How did you end up as a pirate?" Denise asked, glaring at her brother.

"I left the others to rescue you," he answered. "Then I found myself at the mercy of some rather unscrupulous characters, then things just escalated once I met her." Karl glanced over at Sophia. "I thought I was going to have to challenge the bounty hunter for you, but it seems that you've done all right as one yourself."

"Surge may eat like a monster," she commented. "But he's a pretty good guy. Besides, I figure my adventure was better than the one you had with the fake princess."

"Last I checked, the one thing fake about Sophia was her arm," said the cat.

Denise stood there with a blank expression for few seconds. "She's a..." For the first time Denise considered that her judgment was wrong. She had jumped to a conclusion about Sophia.

Denise turned to look at Sophia. "A real...?"

"Second in line to the Neith throne," Karl stated.

"One of the last descendants of the Ruby Eyed Empress," Lightening added.

"Where the hel- " Denise paused for a moment and caught herself, "heck did you find a real princess?"

"He bought her off a slave ship," answered the tabby.

"Lightening," Karl whispered, "why did you have to say it like that?"

The hatch to the shuttle slid open, and Karl reentered the vessel for the first time since his sister had disappeared. The three of them followed the cat to a panel with the sound of tapping coming from behind it.

Karl touched a crystal beside it and the panel snapped open ejecting the entangled Justin and Jacob onto the floor.

179

"Thank you so much!" exclaimed Justin, as the two pushed away from each other.

"What are we going to do with these two?" asked Karl.

"We'll do anything you want. Just don't send us back to those crazy people!" Jacob pleaded. "They were planning to turn us into cyborg super soldiers."

The two women both looked down at the men on the floor for a few moments.

"But I guess I can take one as a butler," Sophia stated, staring at Justin.

"And I'll take whichever one is less annoying, as an assistant cook," Denise commented.

"Whatever," Karl said, not wanting to get involved in the decisions of the women about the household staff.

Karl reached inside his pocket and pulled out his handheld.

"Oracle, lay in a course for where the *Lady Eris* and the *Draco* are."

"And once again the day is saved," said Lightening, "thanks to Lightening the cat, and his human helpers. Time for supper."

Published by Ruskras Corner

By Deborah DR Kralich

Historical Fiction-
The Mystery of the Missing Persons

Mysteries-1900s era
Murder as the Organist Plays

1700s era
The Mystique Woven in Our Land

Lt. Plate Series- 1980s era
An Innovative Murder for the Season
The Ruler of the Toys
A Kaleidoscope of Masquerades
The Unknown Puppeteer

By Carl S. Kralich

Science Fiction-
Karl Sabers- Space Knight series
3748 A.D.- The Return of the Cat
Short Stories
The Precious Cargo -published in the anthology- *Bridges*
Coming soon-
The Zodiac War

Made in the USA
Middletown, DE
21 June 2023

32519739R00106